'You don't have to stay down there. I'm well and truly cured of that particular vice. You won't corrupt me if you smoke in my presence.'

Hannah shuddered. Maybe she wouldn't corrupt him, but being with Jack might well corrupt her. Once again she'd failed to tell him the truth, and she knew the reason why. She wanted him to go on wanting her, wanted him to keep looking at her as he just had, wanted to wallow a while longer in his admiration and desire.

It was wicked of her.

And downright dangerous.

Love can be full of surprises!

This is the second book in Miranda Lee's bewitching trilogy *AFFAIRS TO REMEMBER*. This popular Australian author brings especially to you three complete stories of love affairs with a difference—there are twists to all the tales that you won't forget!

AFFAIRS TO REMEMBER by Miranda Lee:

A KISS TO REMEMBER
A WEEKEND TO REMEMBER
A WOMAN TO REMEMBER (coming next month)

Miranda Lee lives near Sydney. Born and raised in the bush, she was boarding-school-educated and briefly pursued a classical music career before moving to Sydney and embracing the world of computers. Happily married, with three daughters, she began writing when family commitments kept her at home. She likes to create stories that are believable, modern, fast-paced and sexy. Her interests include reading meaty sagas, doing word puzzles, gambling and going to the movies.

A WEEKEND TO REMEMBER

BY
MIRANDA LEE

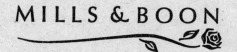

MILLS & BOON

MILLS & BOON and the Rose Device
are trademarks of the publisher.
Harlequin Mills & Boon Limited,
Eton House, 18-24 Paradise Road, Richmond, Surrey TW9 1SR

© Miranda Lee 1996

ISBN 0 263 79422 9

Set in Times Roman 11½ on 12 pt.
01-9603-45972 C1

Made and printed in Great Britain

CHAPTER ONE

A LIGHT drizzle started falling soon after the road began its long winding route up the Blue Mountains. Hannah flicked on the windscreen wipers and glanced over at her passenger.

He was still sleeping, thank heavens. The drive from Sydney up to the cottage was difficult enough at the best of times. On a Friday evening, in the dark and in the rain, it was downright dangerous.

Her hands tightened on the steering-wheel, her stomach muscles following suit. What in hell was she doing? Common sense told her to turn round and go back, take Jack home, confess all and throw herself on his mercy.

I'm terribly, terribly sorry, she could hear herself saying. I don't know what came over me, but of course I'm not your fiancée. Just a very worried secretary who simply couldn't let that cold-hearted ambitious bitch take you for another ride. When that tile fell on your head this morning and you lost the last six weeks from your memory—including your whirlwind romance—I thought at first that might be the end of Felicia. But then a nurse at the hospital said a fiancée had been mentioned and would I please call her. In my mind's eye I saw Felicia swanning in and winning you all over again with her looks and her lies, so before I knew it I'd opened my stupid mouth and said *I* was your fiancée.

Hannah's heart almost jumped into her mouth when Jack shifted in his seat and muttered something under his breath. She sighed with relief when he settled back again, his head lolling to one side, his eyes still shut.

God, for a second there, she thought she'd been speaking out loud instead of in her head. As much as common sense kept ringing warning bells over her reckless deception, no way was she going to heed them.

She didn't care if she lost her job over this.

And she probably would.

Hannah was determined that till Jack got his memory back—the doctor had said that that could happen at any time during the next few days—the only person with him would be herself. She was determined to keep that two-timing witch out of the picture till she could tell Jack the whole appalling truth about the woman he'd been going to marry at the end of the month.

As it stood, dear Felicia was probably at this very moment fuming over the fax from Jack saying that he was having second thoughts about their engagement, and that he was going away for a few days to think things over. The fax also added that she was not to try to contact him, and that he would contact her when he returned.

Any guilt Hannah felt over doing such an outrageous thing, including forging Jack's name, was cancelled when she thought of what she had discovered last night. That woman deserved no consideration. None at all.

Hannah shuddered to think how close she had come to not going to Jack's engagement party and finding out the truth. She'd arrived home from work yesterday to be greeted by her final divorce papers in the mail, which hadn't exactly put her in the mood for partying. She'd literally had to force herself to dress, then drive down to Kirribilli, where the party was being held in a fancy high-rise unit overlooking the harbour, courtesy of a property developer friend of Jack's.

Even before knowing what she knew now, Hannah had harboured misgivings about Jack's choice of bride. She'd only met Felicia a couple of times in a very casual way at the office, but she had just known the woman wasn't right for Jack.

It wasn't jealousy on her part. Hannah had only been Jack's secretary for a little over a year, and there was nothing between them but a strictly work-related relationship. Her feelings for Jack Marshall stopped firmly at liking, respect and gratitude. Oh, yes…she was grateful to him. *Very* grateful.

When she'd applied for the job as private secretary to the boss of Marshall Homes, Hannah had honestly thought she hadn't stood a chance. Good Lord, it had been years since she had used her secretarial skills outside of the home.

But it seemed that Jack had been looking for someone mature, who could be relied on, not some flighty young flibbertigibbet—his word, not hers—who would leave either to go overseas, get married or have babies. She'd assured him she would do none of those things, since she hated travel, had already been married one time too many, and had had babies—two boys, now thirteen and fourteen, both in boarding-school.

Hannah had been so proud of herself when Jack had rung the next day to tell her she had the job.

Pride was something she'd been deficient in for quite some time, and in gratitude for the chance he'd given her Hannah gave him absolute loyalty in return. In her eyes, Jack could do no wrong. He deserved the best, in her opinion, and the best was not a two-faced two-bit soapie-star by the unlikely name of Felicia Fay.

Hannah's top lip curled in contempt at the mere thought of the woman.

Really, she was beneath contempt—the worst excuse for a woman Hannah had ever met. She'd begun to suspect as much the moment Jack's fiancée had opened the apartment door to her the previous evening . . .

'Well, if it isn't the efficient Hannah, running late for once. Whatever will Jack say!'

Startled by her sour tone, Hannah's hazel eyes blinked wide for a second, before narrowing to appraise further the woman her boss was to marry in four weeks' time.

There was no doubt that Felicia was physically beautiful—more so tonight than ever before. She looked a million dollars, in fact. Masses of blonde streaked tresses framed a perfectly made-up face before cascading down over slender shoulders. Her tall model-like figure was encased in a suede trouser suit in a deep blue which complemented her big blue eyes. A long rope of real-looking pearls hung between her high, firm breasts, matching drop earrings swinging sexily from her lobes as she tipped her head to one side and returned the appraisal.

'I see you haven't had time to change,' she drawled. 'I must tell Jack not to work you so hard. Poor Hannah. Still ... black always looks well on older women, doesn't it? It's kind on the complexion and so slimming.'

Poor Hannah was stunned into silence by such an ill-concealed display of bitchiness. The black dress she was wearing was understated but definitely after-five—not the sort of garment she would ever have dreamt of wearing to the office. And her shoulder-length brown hair was stylishly done up in a French roll, not the simple topknot she favoured for work. Despite all this, Hannah knew she didn't hold a candle to the bright butterfly standing before her. So why the attempt to put her down?

'I must thank you for the sweet little engagement gift you sent via Jack,' the butterfly swept on, with a cloying smile. 'One can't have too many ornaments, can one?'

Hannah tried not to choke. The 'ornament' she'd sent had been a very elegant and very expensive Lladro!

'Now, don't just stand there, Hannah, looking out of place. Do come in. Jack's busy talking to some important people at the moment, so you'll have to mingle, I'm afraid.'

Hannah absorbed all the subtle and not-so-subtle slights of Felicia's welcome with a rueful dismay. This was the first time she'd been alone with Jack's fiancée for more than a minute, and the cat's claws were well and truly out. Rather telling, Hannah thought, since she was hardly the sort of secretary to worry a prospective wife. The woman had to be a natural bitch, who believed all other women were the same.

'I don't mind mingling,' Hannah returned as Felicia shut the door behind her.

'Don't you? Funny, I always think of you as such a shy little thing. It amazes me sometimes why Jack has so much confidence in you. You don't seem the type to be a super-secretary.'

Hannah bristled. 'What type would you say I am?'

Felicia's laugh was light and tinkling. Presumably it was meant to soften the malice behind the words. 'Oh, you know. The little-woman-at-home type. You are married, aren't you? You wear a wedding-ring and I heard someone call you Mrs Althorp the other day.'

The fingers of Hannah's left hand automatically curled over into a tight, tense fist. 'Actually, no, I'm not any more,' she said tautly. 'My divorce came through today. I just haven't bothered to take off my rings. Maybe I never will. With the number of males who come through the office, sometimes it's handy to be thought of as married.'

Felicia's glance was sharp. 'So you've become a man-hater, have you?' she asked hopefully.

'I wouldn't say that, exactly. But I have no intention of ever remarrying, if that's what you're asking,' she added, hoping to put the woman's unfounded fears at rest.

Her smile still had an edge to it. 'In that case, I'll make sure I call you Mrs Althorp when I'm in the office. Funny, I know a plastic surgeon called Althorp. Has a practice on the North Shore. But of course, he can't be *your* Althorp. Such a handsome, charming, cultured man.'

Hannah could hardly believe the venom she was hearing. What had she ever done to this woman but be polite and pleasant?

'I must get back to Jack. You can look after yourself, can't you?'

With gritted teeth, Hannah agreed that she could, all the while wondering if dear Felicia was the twenty-nine she claimed to be. Hannah's ex-husband was a dab hand at facelifts, and all sorts of other cosmetic surgery. Dwight's practice depended largely on ladies in the public eye who wanted to look young forever, and other poor put-upon women whose husbands and boy-friends wanted them to look like the models in *Playboy* magazine.

The epitome of feminine desirability these days seemed to be large-breasted, tiny-waisted, slender-hipped, tight-buttocked, firm-thighed, long-legged, small-nosed, big-lipped, wide-eyed, no-wrinkles, clear-skinned beauties, with the public sweetness of angels and the private talents of whores.

Hannah didn't quite qualify. Admittedly when she'd married Dwight, at nineteen, she'd been very pretty and her figure excellent. She was still pretty enough, she supposed, with neat features and nice big eyes. And, being fairly tall, she still looked good in clothes. But the birth of two boys by the time she'd been twenty-one, plus another fourteen years, had taken a certain toll. As for her talents in the bedroom... Well, least said, best said about that.

Felicia, however, obviously did qualify—in every way. Her face and figure were second bar none. Her public demeanour in front of Jack was feminine and accommodating. As far as her private demeanour was concerned... Hannah had no doubt that Felicia's talents in the bedroom were superb as well, to have Jack doing what he'd vowed never to do. Getting married.

Hannah sighed. God, she just hated to think of Jack married to that woman! Felicia was like this apartment—all surface glamour and glitz, but with no soul. In a way, she reminded Hannah of Dwight. Both of them were social climbers, who cared more for appearances than anything else. Jack would find no more happiness with Felicia as his wife than Hannah had with Dwight as her husband.

But it was none of her business, was it, whom her boss married? He was a grown man, thirty-four years old, with a mind of his own. If she dared venture an adverse opinion of his new fiancée, he wouldn't be at all pleased. It might even reverberate on her and the job she valued. Really, there was nothing for it but to smile sweetly and keep her mouth firmly shut.

Hannah moved from the marble-floored foyer down three cream-carpeted steps and into the first of the large living-rooms. It was peppered with small groups of people, all with drinks in their hands, several with cigarettes as well. She cringed as the smoke haze teased her nostrils, setting off that old tell-tale pang of need. Irritated with herself, she swept a flute of champagne from the tray of a passing waiter and pressed it to her lips, taking a few swift sharp swallows. It wasn't as good as a cigarette, but it was better than nothing.

Glancing around, she quickly spied Jack across the heads in the next room. Nothing strange about that. At six feet six inches tall, Jack's head usually stood above all others. His longish wavy jet-black hair was hard to miss as well. Hannah stood, sipping her drink and quietly watching him from a distance.

Not a classically handsome man, Jack never-theless had a face one remembered, with its large, strong features, deeply set blue eyes, squared jaw and uncompromising mouth. One also remembered the scar that ran from his left eyebrow across his cheekbone to his left ear—the result of a run-in with a knife when he was a lad. Or so the rumour went.

Looking at him objectively, Hannah had to concede that a pretty boy, Jack wasn't. But, with shoulders and a body to match his height, he was physically a very impressive and intimidating individual.

She could still remember catching her breath in surprise when, during her job interview, Jack had suddenly stood up to attend an incoming fax. Prior to that he'd been leaning back in his swivel-chair, his long legs stretched out under the desk. She hadn't realised how tall he was. Even now, when he strode into the office some mornings, she could still be awed by his size.

Hannah was not used to physical men. Dwight possessed an elegant, slender frame—nothing like Jack, who was a big bull of a man. No, not a bull—a bear. But, like a lot of big bears, under-neath all the huff and bluff, lay a soft heart.

Too bad it had to be snared by the likes of Felicia.

Hannah moved through the archway which separated the two rooms, her eyebrows lifting in surprise once Jack came into full view. For he was dressed as she had never seen him before, in a sleek black dinner suit with satin lapels that would have done an ambassador proud.

Hannah stared, amazed that Felicia had persuaded Jack to wear what he always called a 'penguin' suit. His usual garb was shorts and a T-shirt if it was hot, jeans and a sweatshirt if it wasn't. Occasionally he sported a pair of casual trousers and a proper shirt if he was going to a restaurant. No tie, though. He despised ties. Yet here he was, with a bow-tie choking his muscular neck.

There was no doubting the power of love!

Or sex, Hannah added with silent cynicism. Men's brains went from their heads to their groins when it came to sex—especially with women who looked like Felicia. Feminine instinct warned Hannah that her boss didn't really love his new fiancée. He was sexually besotted, that was all. As for Felicia... Hannah felt certain that she didn't love Jack either.

But there was nothing she could do about it.

Hannah stopped her progress towards her boss once she saw who Jack was talking to. It was Gerald Boynton, the owner of this unit and a highly successful property developer. About forty, he was one of those sleazily handsome men, with slicked back hair, a pencil-thin moustache and dark oily eyes which slid all over you.

Hannah couldn't stand a bar of him.

Recently he'd bought great tracts of land around the Wyong area, and wanted Jack to build his quality homes on the various developments he had planned. He insisted that together they would 'revolutionise' housing on the Central Coast.

That was the way Gerald Boynton talked. Very big. Still, there was no doubt he got things done, and it looked as if Jack would sign up with him. Hannah felt that it was the second dubious partnership her boss was about to enter into.

The urge to have a cigarette consumed her again, and she swivelled round to see whom she could cadge a cigarette from. The need quickly became a compulsion. Her fingers itched. She licked dry lips. It had been two whole months since she'd gone cold turkey, and she'd hoped she'd moved beyond this. It was clear that she hadn't.

Giving in to temptation with a rush of rebellion, she headed straight for a group of smokers, only to have someone grab her by the arm and pull her to a halt.

'Oh, no you don't,' a deep male voice growled.

Hannah whirled to find Jack glaring down at her from under beetling brows, his piercing blue eyes carrying reproach.

'No, you don't, what?' she tried, but her own eyes were smiling ruefully. When Jack had first noticed she'd given up cigarettes he'd declared himself her watchdog, he himself having only given up the dreaded vice a few months before. His vocal pride in her success so far had always stopped her sneaking one behind his back. Till tonight.

'Hannah, Hannah,' he sighed. 'I can read you like a book. You were coveting that fellow's cigarette over there like a starving man covets a Big Mac. Admit it. I caught you just in time.'

'Yes, boss,' she sighed back. 'I admit it. I was about to become a fallen woman.'

He smiled a wry smile, showing big white teeth within his wide, strong mouth. 'Not you, Hannah.'

'Yes, me,' she insisted, but laughingly.

'You two seem to be having a good time together,' Felicia said as she snaked her arm through Jack's. 'Is it a private joke, or can any old fiancée join in?'

'Hannah was about to have a cigarette,' Jack told her in all seriousness.

'So? She's entitled to, isn't she? You're only her boss, Jack, not her keeper.'

Was Hannah imagining things, or had she just seen the first chink in Felicia's acting ability in front of Jack? She could have sworn there had been a veneer of acid coating the woman's supposedly light words.

'I know how hard it is to give up smoking,' Jack said. 'Hannah needs someone to keep tabs on her.'

'What a sweetie you are, Jack,' Felicia said, reaching up to kiss him on the cheek. 'After we're married, we'll *both* keep tabs on her!' This with a sly look Hannah's way.

Hannah only just managed to stop herself from pulling a face at Felicia in return. Why, oh, why didn't men see through this type of female? It wasn't as though Jack was naïve where women were concerned. Heck, no. There'd been a steady trail of girlfriends over the past year. Still, one had to concede that a woman like Felicia didn't come along every day of the week.

Hannah endured the next hour of the party with great difficulty. Felicia spirited Jack out of her company in no time flat, leaving her to 'mingle' again, which wasn't all that easy. Really, this was a party of Felicia's friends, not Jack's. There was not a single employee present from Marshall Homes other than herself. She began to wonder why Jack had insisted she come. On top of that, everyone she spoke to and who spoke to her seemed to be smoking—several of them offering her cigarettes. In the end she couldn't bear it any longer, and accepted one.

Feeling guilty, and terrified that Jack would see her, she slipped out on to one of the two balconies the unit opened on to. Being midwinter, and with a cool breeze blowing at this height, none of the guests had availed themselves of either. Hannah had to huddle into an alcove to keep the cigarette alight, turning her back to the wind as she puffed away like mad. Oh, how soothing it felt! But how wickedly weak it made her feel!

Dwight's repeated criticism over her many failures to give up smoking permanently popped back into mind, making her drag even more deeply. To hell with you, she thought savagely.

And to hell with that blonde bimbo you replaced me with!

When she heard the sound of a glass door sliding open, Hannah almost died. Fearing it was Jack, come to spring her, she quickly squashed the cigarette underfoot, then squatted down behind a leafy rubber tree. Not daring to breathe, she was waiting for her boss to discover her guilty quaking self when a low moan broke the cold night air.

Hannah froze as more telling sounds met her ears. Dear heavens, someone was kissing, or making love, or doing something decidedly sexual. How embarrassing if they found out she was there, listening to them!

Hannah almost groaned aloud when she heard the woman say 'darling' on a husky whisper. For it was Felicia. The thought of being a silent witness to Jack and that woman doing and saying intimate things made her skin crawl.

'You like that, darling?' she murmured.

'God, Felicia, what am I going to do without you?'

Hannah snapped to attention. For the man wasn't Jack!

'You'll survive, Gerald. You do have your new little mistress to keep you satisfied, after all.'

'She's not a patch on you in bed.'

'Such a flatterer, you are,' Felicia cooed. 'You're rather good yourself. I've never met a man with your style and imagination.'

'Then why the hell are you going to marry that big oaf? He's all brawn and no brains. I wish to hell I'd never introduced you to him. You can't possibly enjoy going to bed with him. I would imagine having Jack on top would be like being run over by a bulldozer. God, don't stop.'

Felicia laughed. 'In that case there must be something to be said for being run over by a bulldozer. Jack might not have your formal education, Gerald, but he's street-smart and not to be underestimated. And what he lacks in imagination he more than makes up for with a quite amazing stamina. I'm not that much a martyr that I would marry a man who couldn't satisfy me in bed.'

'I'd be quite happy to keep on satisfying you. Any time. Anywhere.'

'Yes, but you won't marry me.'

'That's because I'm already married. God, I'll pay you, if that's what you want.'

'Not enough, darling. Under that supposedly magnaminous façade you wear, you're the original Scrooge.'

'I didn't get rich by being stupid.'

'Neither will I. Modelling and acting hasn't brought me any real fame or fortune, and my looks won't last forever. I'm going to marry Jack Marshall, and there's nothing you can say or do to stop me. He's the ideal husband for me. A multi-millionaire. A self-confessed workaholic. And a man who doesn't want children. What more could I possibly hope for? Now, I really must go. Jack will be out of the bathroom by now.'

'But you can't leave me like this,' Gerald groaned.

When Felicia laughed, Gerald told her where she could go in decidedly obscene terminology. Felicia laughed again before opening the glass door and going back inside. Gerald must have quickly followed, because all of a sudden the balcony was very silent and very, very cold.

A shudder of revulsion ran through Hannah. Now the matter was settled. She could not let Jack marry that revolting woman. She wouldn't say anything tonight, but first thing tomorrow morning she would take Jack aside and tell him all she had overheard...

I would have, too, Hannah reminded herself valiantly now, as she glanced over at her sleeping boss again. If Jack had come straight downstairs into the office this morning. If he hadn't gone off instead to the site of the exhibition village Marshall Homes were building at Cherrybrook. And if that damned tile hadn't hit him on the head, knocking him unconscious and obliterating the last six weeks from his mind.

Lord, she could still see the shock on Jack's face when she'd announced their new relationship. If his head hadn't been aching so much, he might have sought to question her further. But his pain, plus his obsessive hatred of hospitals, had obviously kept all the questions she had seen in his eyes from finding voice at that time. His one and only objective had been getting out of there. Then, once in her car, the sedating painkiller the doctor had prescribed had taken over and he'd drifted off to sleep. He hadn't even woken when she'd made the stops required to complete her outrageous plan.

Now Hannah began to wonder just how long he was going to be out of it. Then she began to worry that it might not be the drugs keeping Jack asleep. Maybe it was a case of severe concussion? Maybe he was going to fall into a coma? Maybe he——

'Oh, hell!' she swore, slamming her foot down hard on the brake as the back of a mud-spattered semi-trailer suddenly materialised through the misty rain. Everyone and everything shot forward when the brakes gripped in the wet, the car slewing wildly. A collision was avoided by mere inches.

Jack was instantly but dazedly awake. 'What in blazes?' he growled, then shot a most disconcerting glance over at Hannah. It was part-pain, part-disorientation, part-disbelief. Gradually the fog seemed to clear from his eyes and he frowned at her. 'What in hell do you think you're doing, Hannah?'

Oh, my God, she thought. He's got his memory back.

CHAPTER TWO

'YOU'RE usually such a good driver,' he added, and Hannah tried not to shudder in relief.

She just wasn't ready for him to get his memory back yet. It was hard enough to cope with his being awake. She knew he'd been dying to ask questions back at the hospital about their supposed engagement. Now nothing was going to stop him.

'Sorry,' she mumbled. 'Didn't see the darned thing. This road's murder in the rain.' She slanted him a hopefully soothing smile. 'We'll be at the cottage soon. Only a few more miles.'

'What cottage is that?'

'Don't you remember? I told you about it back at the hospital, when the doctor insisted that if you were fool enough to discharge yourself then the least you could do was to go somewhere quiet and rest for a few days. When I mentioned the holiday cottage I owned in the Blue Mountains up near Leura, he said that would be perfect.'

'I can't really remember. I think at the time I was still too stunned by our engagement to take much in. Besides, I would have blindly agreed to anything to get out of that bloody hospital. So how did you come to own this mysterious cottage? You've never mentioned it before.'

'Dwight bought it several years ago as a getaway. It was part of my divorce settlement.'

'I see. Well, that explains why I didn't know about it. You never talk about your marriage or your husband. Or you didn't before I lost my memory,' he muttered disgruntedly.

Which was pretty true, although Jack did know that Dwight was a doctor. And she *had* told him one day about the apartment she lived in, which was right in the middle of Parramatta's business district, and far beyond a secretary's salary. It was in a fairly new and prestigious building; the lower floors were devoted to shops and offices, and the upper floors housed exclusive executive apartments.

Dwight had bought one of these apartments only a couple of weeks before Hannah had left him. And had arrogantly—but stupidly, as it turned out—put it in her name for tax reasons. He hadn't even had time to put tenants in when she'd walked out on their marriage and laid legal claim to it. It had given her a small amount of satisfaction that there hadn't been a darned thing Dwight could do about it.

As it turned out, it was an ideal spot for her to live, despite Parramatta being a long way from the northern suburb of Mosman, where she'd lived all her married life. Her boys, of whom she had joint custody, were only a short distance away at Kings College, and it was only a ten-minute drive from Parramatta to Marshall Homes' head office at Castle Hill.

'Have you brought me up here before?' Jack asked abruptly, dark puzzlement in his voice.

Hannah tensed. 'No, I haven't,' she admitted.

Jack glanced at his wristwatch, his head snapping up and round in surprise. 'Good God, it's almost eight o'clock!'

'You've been asleep for hours. How are you feeling, by the way?'

'I've felt better.' His hand came up to touch the top of his head carefully.

'You don't feel nauseous, do you?' the doctor had asked her to watch for nausea and vomiting as a sign of a more serious concussion, making her promise to take Jack to a hospital if that happened.

'No,' he denied. 'Just headachy. It's not nearly as bad as it was, though.'

'Do you...er...still think it's May, and not July?'

'Fraid so. And I still can't believe you and I are engaged,' he added, shooting her a much sharper look. 'Hell, Hannah, how and when exactly did that happen?'

A wave of guilty heat filled her face, but she doubted he could see it. It was pitch-black outside, and the light inside the car was dim. 'Er...only this week, actually,' she said.

'Yeah, right, but *how* did it happen?'

Hannah decided that she had to take control before things got really sticky. 'Look, Jack, I realise our engagement has come as a big shock to you. Frankly, it came as a big shock to me too.

One minute you were just my boss, then something happened, and suddenly I just…we just…'

Hannah wanted to groan her dismay. This was her taking *control*? Lord, why hadn't she thought out a believable story to tell him? There again, *was* there a believable story to tell him?

'We became physically involved with each other?' he prompted.

The lack of surprise in his voice sent her eyes jerking round to blink at him.

'That's not the part I can't believe, Hannah,' he said drily. 'I always did fancy you.'

Hannah swung her stunned eyes back on the road ahead, before she really ran into the truck in front of them.

'It was our getting engaged that shocked me,' Jack went on. 'Or, more to the point, your agreeing to marry me. You've told me more than once you'd never get married again. Frankly, I always believed you wanted nothing more to do with men—in that way or any way at all! So what happened to change that?'

She struggled to find her voice, but her mind was still reeling from Jack's bald announcement that he'd always fancied her. She found it hard to believe—but why would he lie?

This highly unexpected revelation gave a totally different meaning to the way he'd looked her over sometimes in the office. She'd always imagined he'd been mentally criticising her fashion sense— as Dwight had done *ad nauseam*. Now she saw him undressing her with his eyes, and suddenly she was all hot and bothered.

'Hannah?' Jack persisted. 'Tell me straight. How did this affair of ours start?'

'I...I don't know. I mean... Oh, God, I don't know what I mean.' She felt totally flustered now, yet she couldn't pull back. The die was cast and she had to roll with it. 'It . . . it happened the day my divorce papers came through,' she invented shakily. 'We...we...worked back late together that night. At one point I became upset. You comforted me and...and one thing just led to another...'

'Are you saying I seduced you at a weak moment?' he demanded disbelievingly. 'Hell, I didn't make you pregnant, did I? Is that why we're getting married? Because you're expecting my child?'

Her face flamed as she blurted out, 'No!' in a panicky voice. This was becoming awful!

Jack frowned across at her. 'I presume by that you mean, no, you're not pregnant.'

'No, I'm not pregnant. And, no, you didn't seduce me either. I . . . I wanted you to make love to me,' she insisted, appalled at herself for letting Jack think that he'd acted dishonourably, then more appalled at the corner she'd backed herself into.

'And once we went from friends to lovers, we actually fell in love?' he suggested. 'Is that what you're saying?'

'Not exactly.' God, this was going from bad to worse!

'Mmm. You mean it's more a matter of compatibility and convenience than runaway romance and passion?'

'I think it's more a matter of stupidity,' she muttered. 'Look, Jack, I think our engagement was rather a rash decision, and I won't hold you to any of it. We haven't even bought a ring yet, so our engagement's easily called off.'

'But I don't *want* to call it off,' he said, astounding her all the more. 'As I said before, I've always been attracted to you. And I like you more than any woman I've ever known. It was only *your* attitude to men and marriage that held me back from trying to deepen our relationship.'

Hannah gave him a startled look before wrenching her eyes back on to the road, her heart racing madly. Dear heaven, where would this all end? It was becoming more crazy by the moment!

'Frankly, my own attitude to marriage has been changing for quite a while,' he went on thoughtfully. 'I'd already come to the conclusion that one steady woman in my life would be much preferable to a series of semi-casual relationships. I don't really have the time to romance one woman after another, and the type who'll go to bed with you *without* romance was beginning to lose attraction for me.'

Hannah refrained from rolling her eyes, thinking to herself that she doubted Felicia had needed much romancing before she'd jumped into bed with Jack. Still, she must be super-dooper in bed, since he had not only asked her to marry him very quickly, but had even taken the whole of last weekend off work to be with her. Unheard of for Jack to do that!

'I must admit it *is* strange, though,' he added, frowning, 'not being able to remember anything about this new intimacy of ours. Damned annoying, actually. I wish I could remember our first time together. I feel I've missed out on something really special.'

Hannah could feel his eyes moving over her, and she blushed fiercely.

'Yes, I'm sure it was very special,' he said slowly, the 'very' seeming to slide down her spine, making her skin break out in goosebumps under her clothes.

Hannah was stunned. She had honestly never considered Jack thinking of her in a sexual context before, and the knowledge that he did was sending her into a spin. She hadn't thought of him in that context either, but suddenly she was very aware of him sitting in the car beside her. His size. His strength. His maleness.

She felt flustered and flattered at the same time.

It had been so long since any man had paid this kind of attention to her—so long since she'd thought of herself as a desirable woman. Dwight had eroded her confidence in her sexuality over the years. Whereas Jack, with his repeated assertions tonight about fancying her, and his hot gaze now roving over her, was very definitely re-vitalising her self-esteem in that regard.

A startling train of thought jumped into Hannah's mind and she sucked in a sharp breath. Jack believes you're his fiancée. He believes you're already lovers. Maybe he'll expect you to go to bed with him tonight as a matter of course?

Dear heavens, she hadn't thought of that!

There she'd been, imagining that she would only have to tuck him into bed, bring hot cocoa and generally play nursemaid till his memory came back. She had never contemplated having to fend off a very virile male who already believed he'd been to bed with her and was wanting to relive what he thought he'd missed.

Hannah had to nip this potential complication in the bud, so to speak, before it blossomed into a full-blown problem.

'If you don't mind, Jack,' she said awkwardly. 'Till you get your memory back, I'd prefer us to resume the relationship we used to have as just secretary and boss. I don't think I'd feel comfortable with anything else just now—what with your not remembering anything about our ... er ... new intimacy.'

'Really? Well, I guess I can understand that, but I sure hope I get my memory back soon,' he muttered testily.

Amen to that, Hannah prayed.

'The doctor said your memory could come back at any time,' she said soothingly.

'The sooner the better,' he grumbled.

A silence descended in the car, which suited Hannah. She was approaching the turn-off, and had to concentrate. Was it around this corner or the next? She wished it would stop raining. It was hard enough to spot in the daytime in fine weather.

The car rounded the corner and, yes, there was the turn-off. Relieved to have done with the highway, Hannah still had to slow appreciably as she turned on to the narrow and bumpy dirt track which led down to the cottage.

The headlights tunnelled through the sleety darkness, showing puddle-filled potholes plus the closeness of the encroaching bushland. They picked up a pair of glassy eyes up in a tree as the road turned. A possum, probably, Hannah thought. Not a koala. Koalas weren't at all nocturnal.

'What an isolated place,' Jack said.

'Actually, we do have several neighbours, but their homes are set back from the road and you just can't see them through the bush.'

'Is the cottage heated? If it isn't, we'll freeze to death.'

'It has two efficient combustion heaters built into the old fireplaces—one in the living-room and one in the kitchen. We'll be warm as toast once I get them going.'

'Won't the wood be wet?'

'I stacked plenty in the laundry when I was up here last weekend,' Hannah informed him without thinking.

'You came up here last weekend?' he immediately pounced, and she could have bitten her stupid tongue off. 'Alone?' he added on a puzzled note.

'Yes, you were busy working,' she said, marvelling at the speed with which she could lie. Not that it was all a lie. He had been busy. Busy having a dirty weekend with the treacherous Felicia, at a guest-house not all that far from here. Hannah had booked it for him herself. 'The place needed airing,' she went on quite truthfully. 'It hadn't been used for a while and I was thinking of bringing the boys up here next school-break.'

'The boys,' Jack repeated thoughtfully, and Hannah wanted to kick herself. Why, oh, why had she brought them up?

Jack swivelled to face her. 'Do Chris and Stuart know about us?'

'No, they don't,' Hannah replied frustratedly. Jack had met her sons during their last school-break, when they'd wanted to come and see where she worked. He had kindly taken them on a tour of the premises and attached exhibition homes, and they'd taken a real shine to him.

'Remember, we only got engaged this last week,' she added. 'Look, Jack, perhaps you should leave all those sorts of questions till after you get your memory back as well, then most of them won't be necessary. I think that would be less complicated and much less wearing all round.'

His sigh showed a very real weariness. 'You're right. I think I'm giving myself another headache trying to work everything out.' And he slumped down in the passenger seat, his head and shoulders drooping.

She slanted him an anxious look. 'Are you sure you feel all right?'

'I'll live.'

'You should be in bed, resting.'

'You could be right.' He began rubbing his temples.

'Won't be long now,' she said, throwing him a motherly smile. 'Here we are, in fact.'

The cottage was old and quaint, made of stone, with a pitched iron roof and two chimneys. It had a small enclosed front porch and front door with stained-glass windows on either side. Inside it had a central hall which opened into two bedrooms and one bathroom on the right, and one long living-room on the left. At the end of the hall was a large, comfy country kitchen, whose large pantry had been converted to a sleekly modern laundry, complete with dryer. Out at the back a wide and sunny veranda overlooked thick bushland, with mountain peaks in the distance.

Two paths led from this back veranda—one leading off on a bushwalk the boys called the Boomerang, because it brought one right back to its starting point, and the other going round the side of the house to a small stone shed which had once housed an old dunny and an equally ancient laundry, complete with copper and washboard. Now it was where the wood, the mower and other various tools were kept.

Hannah loved the place—its simplicity and its peace and quiet. The boys had always liked it too—especially the bushwalking. She'd come up here with them as often as she could after Dwight had bought it, mostly without her husband. He had always seemed to find some excuse not to come at the last minute. Hannah had suspected he was having affairs back then, but had turned a blind eye to it till the day had come when she had been forced to face her cowardice and make a stand.

Recalling her husband's infidelity renewed her resolve to do whatever she could to stop Jack from marrying that amoral woman. She would let Jack believe what he liked about their relationship provided he stayed up here with her, alone and away from Felicia's influence. Of course, that didn't include sleeping with him. That was carrying gratitude too far!

Gritting her teeth, Hannah pulled the car up next to the front steps and switched off the ignition.

'You go on inside,' she told Jack briskly.

'There's a big brass key in the geranium pot on the top step which opens the front door. Your bedroom will be the first on the right. I'll get your things.'

He frowned. 'When did you get my things?'

'While you were asleep. Come, now, no more questions, remember? Just accept I have everything in hand.'

'My ever-efficient Hannah,' he said, opening his door. 'How did I ever manage before you came along?'

Hannah knew what he was referring to. She often did little domestic chores for him, like delivering and picking up his dry-cleaning. She also took care of his personal bills, which he had a tendency to overlook when he was busy on a new project.

'At least now I'll never have to manage without you again,' he said, his smile disturbingly tender.

Hannah sat, transfixed, when he unexpectedly leant back over and took her mouth with his in an incredibly gentle kiss. The softly sensuous contact of his lips brushing hers sent little shivers of delight running up and down her spine. She stared at him as his head lifted, stared deep into those deep blue eyes, true panic welling up within her.

No, no, came the frantic thought. I can't allow this kind of thing to happen. It's not fair to him, or to me. I must speak now—tell him the truth before it's too late.

But then he kissed her again, not quite so gently, and immediately she lost the plot. Common sense kept telling her to keep her lips shut, but her lips didn't seem to be connected to her brain.

His tongue swept deep into her mouth, and she felt it all the way down to her toes. When she moaned, his hands cupped her face, holding it captive as his kiss grew more and more demanding. And more and more seductive. Hannah ached to surrender to its heat, and to its promise of more to come. It had been so long since she'd been kissed like this. *Too* long, obviously.

Guilt finally fought its way through Hannah's scrambled thought-processes, and she wrenched her mouth away from his, pulling back out of his grasp. 'No, stop!' she gasped. 'I can't let you do this.'

'Why not?' he returned thickly.

Because I don't love you, she could have said. Because you're not my fiancé. Because my response comes from nothing but years of frustration and neglect.

But Jack wasn't in a fit state for the truth tonight. And neither was she. Maybe in the morning.

'Your... your headache,' she said instead.

'What headache?'

'Jack, stop it. You promised. I...I can't handle this just now. And neither can you. The doctor said you had to rest. You might be suffering from concussion. The last activity you need is anything to get your blood pressure up. Surely this can wait till you're better?'

Jack let out a shuddering sigh. 'You're no doubt right. But damn it all, Hannah, I can't seem to stop thinking about you, and what it must be like between us. Hell, it must be incredible to have propelled us into a level of caring and commitment that didn't exist six weeks ago. Surely you can understand my curiosity...'

Everything inside Hannah tightened when Jack reached out to lay a tender hand against her cheek. His blue eyes, normally so cool and businesslike, washed over her with a passionate warmth which had a decidedly heating effect on her blood.

'Now that I've had a small taste of what's to come,' he said, 'I have to admit my impatience to have you in my arms. Besides, I rather like the idea of making love to you while I can't remember. It would be like experiencing our first time over again.'

'Jack, please don't make it hard for me to keep saying no,' she pleaded, and meant it. For, astonishingly, she *was* tempted to go to bed with him.

It wasn't love, or even lust, she believed. To be honest, Jack wasn't her physical type at all. She'd always been attracted to fair-haired, smoothly elegant men like Dwight. It had to be because she just wanted to be wanted. Wanted to be needed. Wanted to be stroked and kissed and told she was desirable and beautiful.

Hannah was amazed—and rather shocked—at how strongly she was tempted to take advantage of the situation she'd created with her impulsive deception. Only the realisation that Jack would eventually get his memory back stopped her. As it was, she was still probably going to lose her job over this. Things had already got further out of hand than she'd ever anticipated.

'This weekend we're just good friends,' she stated stiffly. 'Nothing more.'

'We'll see, Hannah,' he muttered, his hand dropping away from her cheek. 'We'll see.'

'I mean it, Jack,' she said, her voice hardening further. 'Till you get your memory back, our relationship is strictly platonic.'

'And what if I said I've already got my memory back?' he tossed back, watching her face all the while.

Hannah was only shaken for a split-second. 'You'd be lying,' she said, quite confidently.

'How can you be sure?'

'I just can.'

'Hmm. Now, I wonder why that is, Hannah, love? What else has happened during the last six weeks to make you sure I'm still in the dark? No, don't tell me. I don't think I want to know. Not tonight. The morning will be soon enough to find out the awful truth. Tonight I think I'd best remain in blessed oblivion.'

CHAPTER THREE

BLESSED oblivion...

I could do with some of that, Hannah thought ruefully as she bent to put another log on the fire.

She stayed on her haunches, staring blankly into the flames, wishing she had never started any of this. It had been a crazy idea. She should have just told Jack the truth right away—all of it— and let him handle the situation with Felicia as he saw fit. He didn't need a mother to hold his hand. He was a grown man.

It had been a mistake in judgement to embark on this ridiculous deception—a silly, impulsive reaction which she hadn't thought through at all properly.

But it was not too late to tell Jack the truth. By morning it might be, however. By then he might well have regained his memory, and he would be furious with her. Not only furious, but suspicious of her motives in doing such a thing. He might even harbour doubts over her story about Felicia and Gerald Boynton, which was the last thing she wanted.

Hannah smothered an exasperated sigh. 'O what a tangled web we weave, When first we practise to deceive!'

'You make a good fire.'

Hannah flinched, then threw a rather stiff smile over her shoulder. Jack was sprawled along one of the two overstuffed sofas which flanked the living-room fireplace, his normally macho-clad frame distractingly clothed in the sleek navy silk pyjamas she'd found in his drawers. He was propped up on one elbow, his hands cupped around a mug of hot chocolate. His feet were bare but not his chin. It was sporting the beginnings of more than a five o'clock shadow.

This was hardly new for Jack. He often didn't shave, sometimes letting two or three days go by before he bothered. Clearly he hadn't bothered this morning. Hannah had always found such inattention to personal grooming unappealing. Dwight had been so meticulous in such matters.

Tonight, however, she found it disturbingly attractive. It seemed to highlight Jack's almost animal-like maleness, the silk pyjamas not really disguising a body more suited to caveman times than the nineties.

All thoughts of telling her boss the truth fled from her mind for a few moments, replaced by memories of how it had felt when he'd kissed her back in the car. She'd tried not to think about that in the hour since they'd arrived, during which time she'd busied herself with all sorts of household chores: lighting both fires, unpacking Jack's clothes, running him a hot bath, making them both some food and drink, showering and changing herself.

Now, all of a sudden, she couldn't stop thinking about her response to Jack's kisses, and what it might feel like to go to bed with him. The realisation that she was undressing him with her eyes and wondering if he was as well-built downstairs as he was everywhere else, really shocked her.

Wrenching her eyes away from him, she busied herself pushing the log right in, then closing and securing the glass door. 'I've had plenty of practice at firemaking,' she said, disguising her inner turmoil under a matter-of-fact voice. 'Not to mention wood-chopping and mowing. Dwight wasn't what you'd call the handyman type.'

Neither had he been a complimenter. It came to Hannah then that Jack was always praising her. She loved that about him.

But she didn't love him. The only man she'd ever loved was Dwight, her husband and the father of her children. No doubt, underneath her hurt and her anger, she was still in love with the rotter!

So why, dammit, couldn't she stop thinking about making love with Jack?

Hannah almost groaned in total exasperation at herself. There was no doubt about it now. She had to tell him the truth. And she had to tell him before things got any further out of hand.

But how? It wasn't going to be easy.

Frowning, she rose from her haunches, wiping her hands down the legs of her jeans before pulling down her jumper from where it had ridden up over her hips.

'I like you dressed like that.'

Hannah's eyes snapped up, blinking her surprise and automatic scepticism. Around the time she had turned thirty Dwight had started saying that her *derrière* was too big to wear jeans, so she'd left all her jeans up here, to wear when Dwight wasn't with her. Admittedly she'd lost weight in the time she'd worked for Jack, but she still found it hard to believe that any man would genuinely fancy her in jeans.

It wasn't her *derrière* Jack was staring at, however, but the thrust of her full breasts against the soft wool of the pink jumper. They tingled beneath his scrutiny, swelling and peaking hard within her bra.

Her body's response both shamed and excited Hannah. God, but it was an eternity since such a thing had happened to her like that—so automatically, so wantonly.

'I like women in casual clothes,' Jack said. 'It makes them look approachable. You've no idea how much more approachable you look in those jeans than the tailored suits you usually wear to work. Mmm, I think I might make jeans your uniform,' he added, then chuckled drily. 'Perhaps not. I'd never get any work done.' Swinging his bare feet on to the floor, he sat up and patted the sofa next to him with his spare hand. 'Come over and sit down. You haven't stopped working since we arrived. It's time you put up your feet.'

Hannah's heart lurched. She stared at him for a few terrifyingly electric moments before panic at the feelings spiralling through her sent her scurrying towards the other sofa. 'I'll just sit over here, I think,' she babbled. 'There's not much room next to you and you might spill your drink.'

'No, I won't,' he said, sliding down to the far corner and depositing the mug on the side-table right next to his elbow. 'Now there's room,' he said, patting the sofa again, his blue eyes glittering with desire as they raked over her breasts once more.

Her panic flared anew. And she must have shown it.

His frown was swift and dark. 'What is it, Hannah?' he asked. 'What's troubling you?'

'Nothing,' she lied, sitting there with her knees clenched together and her hands nervously massaging her thighs. 'Nothing.'

'You can't honestly expect me to believe that. Your face is an open book, if one wants to take the time to read it. Something's definitely wrong,' he insisted, his penetrating blue eyes giving her no mercy.

He moved forward to perch on the edge of the sofa, his hands on his knees. 'Look, Hannah, I know I said I didn't want you to tell me any nasties till the morning, but I can see neither of us will sleep properly if the air isn't cleared. So out with it,' he commanded in his most effective 'boss' voice. 'What *else* has happened during the last six weeks which has you all tied up in knots?'

She grimaced, knowing that this was the chance she'd been looking for—the opportune moment to unburden her conscience. All she had to do was open her mouth and let the truth spill out.

But it just wasn't that easy. Not at all. Her head whirled and her tongue felt thick. She couldn't seem to find the right words. Or any words at all!

Her stricken expression brought an answering anxiety to his face.

'My God, it's not the business, is it?' he burst out, his head snapping up, his knuckles going white as his large hands gripped his knees. 'I haven't somehow stuffed it up, have I? I could bear just about anything, but not that. I've worked too long and too hard to start at the bottom of the heap again.'

Hannah's heart went out to him. She'd heard the stories about his childhood in a state institution for orphans, how he'd left to strike out on his own at fourteen, a boy with the body of a man, how he'd worked as a builder's labourer and learnt his trade by trial and error. He'd started small, buying a single block of land, building a house on it and selling it as a package, then using the profit to buy *two* blocks of land, repeating the process till he'd become one of the biggest home-builders in New South Wales.

Hannah could appreciate Jack's panic. In his shoes, she'd have felt exactly the same.

His obvious distress had the effect of her finding her voice. To a degree.

'Nothing bad's happened to the business, Jack,' she insisted fiercely. 'Truly. If you must know, I... I...' Once again her voice dried up, her courage failing her anew.

'What?' he demanded impatiently. 'For God's sakes *what*, Hannah?'

It was no use. She just couldn't tell him the truth. Not yet. Not tonight.

'I... I've failed, Jack,' she blurted out instead, jumping to her feet. 'At giving up smoking. I... I'm sorry but I just didn't make it. Now I simply *have* to have a cigarette!' Which was true. Anything to calm the nerves that were tap-dancing all through her body. 'I think I left a packet out in the kitchen,' she said, and promptly fled the room.

'And there I was, thinking something disastrous had happened,' he called after her, an amused chuckle betraying his relief.

Hannah groaned her dismay once she reached the kitchen, her trembling hands lifting to pick up several strands of hair which had come loose from their topknot. She stuffed them back in, then rummaged through the drawers till she did indeed find a packet of cigarettes, plus some matches. Her excuse had quickly become a reality. A cigarette was definitely needed.

Putting one between her lips with shaking fingers, she finally lined the end up with an equally shaking match, then drew in deeply.

'You don't have to stay down there in Coventry,' Jack called out drily. 'I'm well and truly cured of that particular vice. You won't corrupt me if you smoke in my presence.'

Hannah shuddered. Maybe she wouldn't corrupt him, but being with him might well corrupt her. Once again she'd failed to tell Jack the truth, and she knew the reason why. She wanted him to go on wanting her, wanted him to keep looking at her as he just had, wanted to wallow a while longer in his admiration and desire.

It was wicked of her.

And downright dangerous.

Jack was not the sort of man to tolerate being teased for long. Hannah wasn't ignorant of the sort of female he'd dated, or the sort he'd finally proposed to. They were all overtly sexual creatures, who dressed provocatively and never bothered to hide the nature of their relationship with the boss of Marshall Homes.

Being Jack Marshall's girlfriend meant one thing and one thing only. Being his fiancée wasn't much different, from what she could see. Felicia had spelt it out to Gerald Boynton. Jack didn't want a family. He didn't want the love of a lifetime. He wanted a bed-partner. Permanent, as opposed to casual. Sooner or later, if she kept up this pretence, he would expect her to sleep with him.

And she wasn't sure she could find the strength to resist him. That was why to go on pretending to be Jack's fiancée was so dangerous.

Hannah drew deeply on the cigarette, knowing what she *should* do, but perversely unable to do it. All she could promise herself was that *she* would not initiate anything. She would stop undressing him with her eyes, keep her distance, and work hard at maintaining the platonic relationship she had asserted they should stick to till Jack's memory returned.

'I...er...I think I'll still stay out here for a while,' she called back, knowing she needed a few minutes' grace to gather herself and recapture some composure.

Two cigarettes and several self-lectures later, Hannah made a brief visit to the main bedroom then returned to the lounge, where she walked over to stand with her back to the fire, determined to act with her usual cool efficiency.

'I've switched your electric blanket down to one,' she told Jack, who was finishing up his hot chocolate. 'I think perhaps it's time you went to bed, don't you? The doctor said you were to rest.'

'I'm resting right here,' he returned, putting the empty mug back on the table. 'In fact, I... I——'

He broke off abruptly with a sharply sucked in breath, both his hands flying up to his temples.

'What is it?' Hannah asked, alarmed. 'Are you in pain?' When he didn't say anything, his eyes squeezing tight as his face screwed up, Hannah flew to sit beside him, her hands fluttering as she didn't know where to put them.

'Can you hear me, Jack? Talk to me, for pity's sake!' she cried.

Slowly his face unravelled, his hands dropping back to his lap as his eyes opened to blink blankly at her. 'That... that was the strangest experience,' he said at last, shaking his head as if to clear it. 'A series of flashes—like images up on a screen. Weird...'

'Images of what?'

'I'm not sure. There were lots of people in a big room. All dressed up. I didn't recognise most of them. Or the place. There was this blonde... dressed in blue. I felt I knew her, but now I can't seem to put a name to the face. Oh, and Gerald was there. Gerald Boynton.'

Hannah gulped. The party. He was remembering the party.

'Have I been socialising with Gerald lately?' Jack asked, still puzzled.

'Not over-much. He did throw you...er...us, I mean, an engagement party the other night. His wife's a blonde,' she said in desperation, aware that she was once again bypassing a chance to tell Jack the truth. 'Maybe that's who you were seeing?'

'Could be. I've never met his wife. Not that I recall, that is. When was this party? And why were we all wearing dinner suits, if it was just a party?'

'It was last night, actually. Thursday. Gerald insisted it be formal.'

Jack snorted. 'Typical Gerald. He's an out and out show-off.'

'Mmm.'

Jack darted her a sharp look. 'You don't like him, do you?'

'Can't say I do. He's what we women call a sleaze-bag.'

Jack frowned. 'He hasn't been making a nuisance of himself, has he?'

'No. I just don't like the way he looks at me.'

Jack laughed. 'Come now, Hannah, you can't blame a guy for looking. You must be used to men looking at you.'

Not really, Hannah thought, still astonished at how much Jack genuinely fancied her. Maybe she was better looking than she'd thought. Or maybe Jack had gone half-blind with that bump on his head.

'Have I agreed to that proposition of his yet?' Jack resumed abruptly. 'You know the one I mean.'

'Yes, I know the one you mean. And no, you haven't. *Yet.*'

'From the sound of your voice, I gather you'd prefer I didn't.'

'I wouldn't presume to tell you what to do, Jack. You're the boss.'

'Not even now that you're the boss's fiancée?' he asked smilingly.

Hannah flushed under Jack's warm and highly seductive tone. As much as she couldn't bring herself to tell him about Felicia, she felt she had to say something which her conscience could cling to, and which would give her some kind of defence later on, after his memory returned. 'As I said earlier, Jack, our...er...engagement was rather a spur-of-the-moment decision. Maybe you'll want to rethink things at some future date?'

'Don't be ridiculous,' he muttered, with a measure of exasperation, reaching out to draw her into his arms before she could escape. 'You're perfect for me in every way, Hannah. We get along. We work well together. You've already had children, so you won't pine for more, and obviously we're sexually compatible. I'm just glad I finally found a way to win you over to the male race again, even if I can't remember it.

'If I'd known you wanted me in that way I'd have seduced you earlier. Oh, yes, I know you said I didn't seduce you, but I have a feeling you're lying about that. I must have, for my Hannah is not a bold woman. She's rather shy in such matters, which pleases me all the more. I've had my fill of bold women.'

Hannah stared at him, appreciating the irony of that statement. If only he knew who he was really engaged to!

'You're such a classy lady,' he went on warmly. 'I can hardly believe that you're attracted to someone like me.'

Hannah's eyes widened when he started to bend his head, obviously intending to kiss her. She couldn't help stiffening in his arms, terrified of where this would end. She hadn't been this flattered or this complimented in years!

Or this excited either.

He stopped, his eyes clouding as they jerked up to frown down at her.

Hannah's stomach turned over. Was he reacting to her reaction, or had he remembered something more?

His hands dropped away from her as he straightened, a wariness entering his frowning eyes.

'Am I being thick here, Hannah?' he asked brusquely. 'Have you been trying to tell me that it's *you* who regrets our engagement? That you're having second thoughts? That you've decided I'm not good enough for you?'

'No!' Hannah exclaimed, her hands lifting to cradle his face before she could think better of it. 'No,' she repeated in a raw whisper as the hurt in his eyes moved her to reassure him.

'I'm not an educated man,' he grated out. 'Nothing like your doctor husband.'

No, he wasn't at all like Dwight, came the rather enlightening realisation. He wasn't arrogant like Dwight, or cruel, or critical. What did an education count for if all it produced was a self-centred, self-important ego, which left no room for anyone's wishes or feelings but their own?

And it wasn't as though Jack wasn't smart. He was. *Very* smart, as even Felicia had pointed out to Gerald Boynton.

'You're nothing like my husband, Jack,' she said, her voice shaking with emotion. 'And I'm glad you're not. You're twice the man he is, or ever could be,' she insisted. And astonishingly, she meant it.

They stared deep into each other's eyes, and gradually she became aware of the stubble beneath her fingers. Her thumbs moved to caress it, to feel the primitive maleness sprouting forth, hard and sharp against the softness of her touch. Something equally primitive began to rise within her. She ached for him to rub his chin against her cheek, to feel its roughness against her breasts and the soft inner flesh of her thighs.

In her mind's eye she saw him do all those things, and everything inside her kicked over. So intense was the feeling this imagined scenario produced that she jerked her hands away from him, but he caught them in his, dragging her heated face back close, forcing her eyes back to his.

'And you, my darling Hannah,' he rasped, 'are more woman than any woman I ever hoped to call my own.'

Hannah tried to feel guilt at his words. Instead her only reaction was a wide-eyed soul-stirring wonder that Jack could feel like that about her. She could hardly believe it.

Tears pricked her eyes.

'Now, what's all this about?' he said gently, kissing the moisture from her eyes and cheeks. 'Were you worried that I might not feel the same way about you just because I'd lost a few miserable weeks of my memory? Did you think I wouldn't still want you?'

A sob caught in her throat as she nodded dumbly, knowing that everything was now totally out of her control. What would be, would be. She was incapable of stopping the flood of feeling washing through her. Dwight might not find her desirable any more, but Jack obviously did. If he wanted her, she would not—could not—stop him.

'Silly Hannah,' he murmured, and, tipping them both back against the sofa, closed the space between their mouths.

'We *are* good together, aren't we?' he whispered thickly after he came up for air. 'Very good.'

Hannah shivered with sensual delight when he held her close and his cheek grazed hers. Her hands slid up over his silk-covered chest, lifting to splay into his glossy black hair, revelling in every sensual moment.

Till she contacted the huge scab on his crown.

When Jack flinched violently she sprang back from him, appalled that she had so quickly forgotten the accident he'd suffered that very morning, plus the doctors' warnings that he should be doing nothing but resting.

'Oh, Jack!' she cried. 'Your poor head. Oh Lord, I forgot! We...we have to stop this,' she said, jumping to her feet. 'You're...you're not well enough for this kind of thing.'

He gave a dismissive shrug. 'My head doesn't hurt that much if you don't touch it. And we were only kissing, Hannah. Still,' he went on a touch wearily, rising to his feet as well, 'perhaps you're right. As much as I'd love to take you to bed right now, I don't think I'd do it justice. I'm sure by tomorrow night I'll be in far better shape.'

'No, Jack,' she derided, finding some common sense now that she was out of his arms. Heavens, but he did have a way with that mouth of his, totally seducing her with just a couple of kisses. Lord, he'd even made her forget that to go to bed with a man one actually had to take off one's clothes!

If she wavered again, she would just have to keep remembering that harrowing and potentially humiliating fact. Once Jack saw her in the nude, he might be as turned off by her imperfections as Dwight had been.

'There won't be any bed together tomorrow night either,' she said, her resolve well and truly strengthened by this last thought. 'We agreed that till your memory comes back we'd keep our relationship platonic.'

'No, Hannah. We didn't *agree* on that at all,' Jack argued back.

'Well that's the way it's going to be!' she insisted. 'Look, for all we know you might have a serious concussion,' she went on, appealing to Jack's common sense. 'I'm not going to risk doing anything that might be dangerous to your health, Jack.'

His sigh was irritable. 'I see you've put your "mother" hat back on, and I know how hard that is to shift. Hell, Hannah, if I ever get the chance to be reincarnated, I think I'll come back as your third son!'

So saying, he stepped forward, took her by the shoulders and landed a very chaste kiss on her forehead. 'Goodnight, Mum. See you in the morning. Who knows? By then, I might even think it's July!'

CHAPTER FOUR

THE morning dawned crisp and clear and cold, a typical winter's day in the Blue Mountains.

Hannah woke with the arrival of watery sunlight through the window, blinking her bewilderment for a moment before she remembered where she was—in one of the boys' single beds, not in the big brass bed in the main bedroom.

It was the first time she'd slept in a single bed since she'd married Dwight over sixteen years ago. The flat she now lived in had come with a queen-sized bed already installed in the main bedroom. For ages Hannah had stuffed pillows down the empty side, till she'd got used to the space and the emptiness of sleeping alone in a large bed. Now she was well used to sprawling over the whole mattress and found a single bed rather confining, though cosy enough on a cold morning.

She toyed with the idea of getting up, but a glance through the window showed a thick frost on the ground, the below-zero temperature confirmed when she put one hand out to check the time and promptly almost shivered to death. Dropping the watch post-haste, she snatched her chilled hand back under the quilt and snuggled down.

So what if it was after seven? So what if she was normally up and about by now?

I'm not getting up, she vowed defiantly. I'm staying here till lunchtime, if need be.

Hannah snuggled down further, pretending to herself that the main reason she wanted to hide in bed was the cold, and not because she didn't want to face Jack. But it wasn't long before her thoughts turned to what had happened the day—and the night—before.

Stupid, she decided. She was stupid! First for pretending she was Jack's fiancée, then for not coming out with the truth once things had started getting sticky. In fact, 'stupid' did not adequately describe her actions. She would have to find a better word.

Dwight would have been able to come up with several, she decided bitterly. Over the years she'd been called illogical, over-emotional, ridiculous, foolish, dumb, even *non compos mentis* on occasions.

Dwight had had no patience with her sometimes sentimental impulses, such as the time she'd picked up a starving but obviously pregnant cat from the street and brought it home. He'd insisted she take the poor frightened animal to the RSPCA. If Hannah remembered correctly, he'd called her tears 'irrational'. So what if the mangy thing was put down? he'd argued irritably. It was probably diseased, and, even if not, Sydney already had too many cats.

Irrational...

That was exactly what he would have called what she had done yesterday. Irrational.

Still, Hannah thought there were *some* excuses for what she'd done. Everything had happened so fast, and her intentions had been good. Surely she wasn't entirely to blame for not seeing that it would all go wrong? How could she have anticipated Jack jumping on the bandwagon of their engagement so enthusiastically? She'd expected him to stay shocked for days, not become smugly pleased. She'd expected him to keep his distance, not be all over her like a rash. She certainly hadn't expected to *like* his being all over her like a rash.

One part of her said that the sensible course of action, for her own sake and the survival of her job, would be to tell him the truth first thing this morning. But the more emotional and decidedly female part of Hannah still didn't fancy risking Jack in Felicia's clutches again, not without his memory intact. The woman was a snake—a poisonous, venomous snake!

She was also an accomplished actress, who could lie her teeth out quite brilliantly without batting an eyelash. She might even succeed in making Hannah look the liar! The vicious bitch would probably accuse her of taking advantage of the situation because she wanted Jack for herself!

No, she could not tell him the truth. Not yet. On Monday, maybe, if he still hadn't got his memory back, because by then she would be forced to.

But that was two whole days away—two whole days of keeping up this pretence which was getting more difficult with each passing moment.

A least she'd put a temporary tin hat on Jack trying to make love to her. But she wondered how long that would last. There was no doubt he genuinely seemed to fancy her, which she still found amazing. Jack had not dated a female less than stunning or over thirty in all the time she'd known him. Frankly, before Felicia, they'd all been closer to twenty than thirty, and all very outgoing, sexy little pieces.

It was to be thanked for, in a way, that she did not possess such sexual confidence. Otherwise she just might have surrendered to Jack's advances last night.

And where would that have led? She shuddered to think.

'Hannah! Where are you? Hannah! Are you there?'

Jack's panicky cries propelled her out of the bed like a shot. Oblivious of the cold, or her bare feet, she raced from the room, down the hallway, past the bathroom towards the main bedroom. Her nightie, thank the Lord, was a roomy neck-to-ankle flannelette number—white with pink flowers on it and a sweet Peter Pan collar with lace edging—which didn't hinder her haste.

Hannah slid down the carpet runner into the open doorway like a hitter into first base, scrambling to keep upright by grabbing the doorframe. 'What is it?' she asked breathlessly, staring at

Jack, who was sitting bolt-upright in the middle of the big brass bed, looking rather wild with his black wavy hair falling all over his face and his chin now dark with a two-day growth. 'Are you ill? Have you got your memory back? What? What?'

He scooped his dishevelled hair back with both hands, his mouth splitting into a wide smile of relief. 'Thank God. For a moment there I thought I was in the middle of a nightmare, or a Stephen King novel. I woke up not knowing where the hell I was. Then everything that happened yesterday came flooding back, and for a few appalling seconds I began to wonder if any of *that* was really real, or just a dream. You're not a dream, though, are you, Hannah? You're quite real.'

'I should think so,' she said, her teeth chattering as she stood there, hugging herself. 'Only real people freeze to death. So you haven't remembered any more of the last six weeks?'

'Not another second, I'm afraid. Damned annoying, isn't it? Maybe I'll never get those six weeks back. Maybe they're gone forever.'

Hannah had never even considered such a possibility, and she didn't like the idea one bit. 'The doctors seemed quite sure you would, Jack,' she said, praying they had been right. 'They said it was just a matter of time—that once the bruising on your brain went away you'd be back to normal.'

'What would they know?' he grumbled. 'You don't honestly think they have amnesia victims wheeled in every day of the week, do you?'

'No, but if you weren't going to get your memory back at all, you wouldn't have even had those flashes last night. Try to be patient and stop worrying. Look, I'll just go and get my dressing-gown on. I'm freezing to death here.'

'Be my guest,' he muttered. 'That's the sort of nightie which a dressing-gown could only improve.'

It was the first critical thing Jack had ever said to her about her appearance and she bristled. 'It happens to be a very nice nightie,' she defended archly. 'And very practical.'

'Oh, I fully agree with you, Hannah. If ever there was a practical nightie, that one's it. It also has "platonic" written all over it!'

'Good,' she snapped. 'Because that's exactly the sort of relationship we're having this weekend.'

'Only till I get my memory back,' he countered, his blue eyes hard as nails. 'That *is* the agreement, isn't it?'

'Absolutely.'

'Well, when that happens—and it can't be too damned soon for my liking—I'm going to use that ghastly bloody nightie to light the fire!'

Hannah almost laughed. The only fire Jack was likely to light after he got his memory back was the fire of his own temper. He wasn't going to be at all happy with her for this pretence. Her

boss had as much of an ego as any other man—
and as much of a temper, as he was displaying
at this very moment. If he thought she'd played
him for a fool in any way, he would really hit the
roof!

'Don't forget what the doctor said about your
blood pressure,' she reminded him sweetly. 'How
about I pop along and get us both some coffee?
You're like me, Jack. You're never yourself in
the mornings till you've had at least three cups.'

It had become something of a joke in the
office, the amount of coffee the boss and his secretary consumed.

'I won't be long,' she said, and scurried off,
happy to escape his grumpy company.

Hannah grimaced as she dragged on her pink
chenille dressing-gown, sashing it loosely around
her waist. Although lovely and warm, it was as
maidenly as her nightie, as were her fluffy pink
lambswool-lined slippers. Hannah hadn't liked
Jack's comment about her nightie, or the way
he'd looked at her in it. She'd much preferred
the flattering way he'd stared at her in her jeans
and jumper last night, and the compliments he's
given her.

Still, she supposed it was wiser not to dress in
any way which might revive his male urges. It
was obvious by his bad mood and his pointed
remarks that he was still feeling frustrated after
last night. She suspected that Jack was one of
those men who didn't like going without sex for
too long.

Dwight wasn't really of that type—which was odd, since he'd been notoriously unfaithful. He could take it or leave it, especially when his mind and energy were occupied on more important things, such as money, power and success. Of course, Dwight liked challenges—and where was the challenge in bedding a wife? Those other little dolly-birds had been ego-boosts, not the result of an unquenchable thirst for sex.

Hannah wouldn't have been surprised if the girl he was now living with, and whom he planned to marry, had been not the object of passion but of ambition and pride. Dwight would get a real kick out of walking into a room with darling Delvene on his arm. For she was incredibly beautiful. Perfection, in fact.

She ought to be, Hannah thought with dry sarcasm. Dwight had operated on her often enough.

Hannah frowned, amazed that she could think of Dwight's betrayals this way, without feeling any real pain, without wanting to burst into tears. Who knew? Maybe she was getting over the hurt at long last.

It was certainly time she did—time to throw off old ghosts and go forward. If nothing else, last night had shown her that she was still a desirable woman with plenty to offer a man. Not everyone, she decided, with a burst of optimism and hope, wanted or expected physical perfection in their partner.

Hannah blinked with pleasant surprise, her new positive frame of mind suggesting to her that the small imperfections of her flesh were really just that. Very small. It was silly to keep being hung up about them because of Dwight's repeated and deliberately demeaning criticisms.

Her breasts didn't really sag all that much without a bra. Her hips were womanly, not wide. As for her stretchmarks... One would have to look darned hard to find them, since they were very low down and had faded over the years from purplish to pale pink.

Now Hannah frowned again. Such thinking might be good for her confidence and self-esteem, but it was downright dangerous to her resolves for this weekend. One of the only reasons she'd stopped Jack making love to her last night had been her negative feeling about her body. If she started thinking more confidently about herself in that way, she might find her boss's desires very hard to resist.

Hannah kept this thought to the forefront of her mind during a quick visit to the bathroom, where among other things she brushed out her hair, then knotted it severely at the nape of her neck. A brutally honest glance in the mirror told her that Jack wouldn't find her too desirable with her hair like that, her thirty-five-year-old face devoid of make-up and her eyes still slightly puffy from sleep.

She hurried out to the kitchen, which was still nicely warm from the combustion stove going most of the night. She was reviving it with a couple of fresh logs when a sensible thought crossed her mind and, after putting on the electric kettle, she marched back down the hall to the main bedroom.

Jack glanced up when she appeared in the doorway, his expression showing that the dressing-gown was as much out of favour as the nightie. 'And *that* little number will go in the charity bin,' he said testily. 'So where's the coffee?'

'Not ready yet. I was thinking, Jack,' she went on, steadfastly ignoring his disapproval in her appearance, 'it's much warmer in the kitchen than here in the bedroom. I couldn't find your dressing-gown when I looked yesterday, but there's an old one of Dwight's in the wardrobe. There's some slippers too, if you want. Why don't you put them on and come down to the kitchen for your morning coffee?'

Jack scowled down at her own slippers, shaking his head before looking up at her face. 'I get it,' he said, nodding wryly. 'This is your "hands-off" uniform. Waste of time, Hannah. I'm not a morning man, anyway. Besides, my head feels like it's full of cotton wool.'

'Perhaps you should take some of those tablets the doctor gave you yesterday.'

'Hell, no. They send me to sleep and make me feel worse. It's not a headache, exactly, just a thickness. It's probably part caffeine withdrawal. I'll get up, like you said, and consume a couple of gallons of coffee.'

'I'll see you shortly in the kitchen, then.'

Hannah couldn't help it. When he walked into the kitchen she almost burst out laughing. Dwight's green checked dressing-gown was several sizes too small and he'd put some striped football socks on his feet in lieu of the slippers, which had undoubtedly proved too small for his big feet.

'If you dare laugh,' he snapped, glaring at her, 'you're fired!'

Hannah covered her mouth with both hands, but her eyes were dancing. Their eyes clashed, and suddenly he grinned at her. Soon, they were both laughing.

'So where *was* your dressing-gown?' she asked when she finally brought the mugs of steaming coffee over to the table, placing one in front of Jack, then carrying her own around to the opposite side of the table. 'I looked everywhere.'

'There *isn't* one,' he informed her, picking up the mug to sip appreciatively. After several mouthfuls, he sighed his satisfaction and put the mug down. 'Great coffee. I never wear a dressing-gown. I don't usually wear pyjamas either. These were a present from some female or other, but they've never been out of the drawer before. I only wore them in deference to your modesty and the cold. My place, as you know, is air-conditioned.'

'Oh,' she said, wishing his words didn't evoke such a vivid picture of him walking around his place in the nude. She fell uncomfortably silent, staring down into her coffee while she sipped.

'So what are we going to do all day?' he asked. 'You can't expect me to just lie around. I'm not a lying around sort of guy.'

Hannah had already thought of things they could do today, but suddenly her perverse mind added another way they could fill in the day. Feeling flustered for a moment, she took another sip of her coffee before putting down her mug and looking up, praying that there was no betraying heat in her cheeks. Jack's cool blue gaze across the table suggested that she was safe—for the moment.

'Well, after we're dressed and have had breakfast,' she suggested, 'I thought we might go on a long, slow bushwalk. That should help clear your head, and it's going to be a lovely day once the sun's well and truly up. Then, after lunch, I thought you might lie down in the sun on the veranda and either read or have a nap. There's a couch out there just made for napping. Then later, if you like, we could drive down to the shops at Leura, buy some take-away and pick up a couple of videos. Or, if you'd prefer, I could rustle up something here and we could just watch whatever's on TV.'

'Mmm. Can't remember the last Saturday I didn't work with Roger and co on-site somewhere. Which reminds me. Do you have a phone here? I'd like to ring Roger and have him fill me in on what's been going on during the past six weeks, building-wise.'

Hannah's stomach curled over. 'No,' she said curtly, panic making her sharp.

'No, what?'

'No, I don't have a phone here, and no, you're not going to ring Roger. The doctor ordered peace and quiet, and peace and quiet is what you're going to get! It's only two miserable days till Monday. Surely you can last two miserable days without Marshall Homes? Do you realise that people think you're a workaholic, Jack? There's more to life than work, you know.'

'I know that,' he growled. 'But the only other activity I enjoy in life has been temporarily banned!'

He glared at her, and she blushed furiously. 'I don't believe that's the only other thing you enjoy in life. If it is, that's a very narrow view, Jack. There are a lot of other things we could enjoy doing as a couple besides sex.'

'Are there, now? And what other things would you suggest I enjoy, Mrs Althorp? Going to the opera, perhaps? Visiting art galleries?'

'There's nothing wrong with enjoying art and music,' she defended hotly, while underneath recognising a degree of hypocrisy.

During her marriage to Dwight, he'd dragged her along to the opera and various trendy galleries all the time. Not because either of them had genuinely enjoyed or appreciated such activities, but because Dwight had thought that that was the thing to do to rise in society.

Hannah had no doubt widened her mental horizons by going, and had learnt a good deal about that kind of music and art. But in all truth, she preferred listening to k d Lang rather than Joan Sutherland, and most modern art left her cold. She much preferred the old masters, or photographic prints, but when she'd said as much to Dwight he'd called her a Philistine of the first order.

But Jack didn't know any of that, and his sarcasm had sounded too much like criticism for her liking. It was the second time he'd criticised her this morning, and it was beginning to upset her.

'You're being very picky this morning,' she snapped. 'And in case you've forgotten, I stopped being Mrs Althorp some time back.'

'Did you? I don't think so, Hannah. I don't think so at all. He's left his mark on you, that bastard. One day you're going to tell me all about that wretched marriage of yours!'

'What makes you think I haven't already?' she flung at him.

Jack was taken aback for a second, sitting back in the chair, blue eyes wide. But then he moved back forward again, his hands cupping his mug, his expression quietly confident. 'Because I just know you haven't,' he said. 'Don't ask me how I know that, but I do.'

'Is that so?' she muttered.

'Yes, that's so. So why don't you tell me now? We've nothing much else to do today, so we might as well talk, don't you think?'

Hannah shrugged, her seeming indifference hiding instant tension. To talk about her marriage would be to hold herself and her inadequacies up to a mirror, which had never made her feel good.

'There's nothing much to tell,' she said brusquely. 'It's an old story. Brilliant working-class boy marries pretty, but not so brilliant working-class girl. He quickly goes up in the world and just as quickly leaves her behind. But by then she's had two children, and so, because he does have some affection for his sons, he tries to make over his unsuitable wife to a more suitable model, befitting his new successful lifestyle.

'Failure is inevitable, because of her unwillingness to co-operate fully, and eventually he starts looking round for someone else—which, of course, requires a lot of sampling before he makes up his mind. Finally he finds a near-perfect specimen, who's only too happy to have her slight imperfections corrected.'

'What imperfections?' Jack intervened, frowning. 'And in what way do you mean...corrected?'

'Didn't I ever tell you Dwight is a plastic surgeon?' Hannah tossed back, her own smile very plastic. 'A brilliant one, of course. He could have made me look twenty-five forever, if I'd have agreed, but stupid me didn't fancy going under the knife to win back his love. Stupid me wanted to be loved for myself.

'Clearly, dear Delvene doesn't have such scruples. Although she was already quite stunning, and only twenty-six, she's had her nose reshaped, her boobs enlarged, plus some negligible fat in her buttocks sucked out. Dwight was closely inspecting this last piece of handiwork in his surgery one day,' Hannah bit out, 'when his stupid wife walked in.

'When he had the gall to bawl me out for interrupting him during the examination of a patient, I pointed out to him—with superb indifference, I thought—that his fly was open. Then I walked out—of the office and of the marriage.'

She gulped down the lump which had filled her throat during this bitter version of her marriage, then glared at Jack's openly sympathetic expression, hating the pity in his blue eyes as they roved over her face. 'If you say, Poor Hannah, or anything like that,' she snapped, 'I'll scream.'

'All right, I won't,' he said, any lingering sympathy in his face so swiftly replaced by a matter-of-fact manner that she was startled out of her self-pitying state.

When he stood up abruptly, Hannah gaped up at him. 'Where are you going?'

'To have a shower and then get dressed. Oh, and don't make my bed for me, thank you. I'm quite capable of doing that for myself. I'm not an invalid. I will let you cook me some breakfast, though. It's hard to cook in someone else's kitchen. Whatever you've got will do fine. I'm not fussy. Then, after breakfast, I think we'll set out on that bushwalk you mentioned. That sounds like just the thing.'

'Just the thing for what?' she asked, feeling both rattled and instantly wary.

'Just the thing for getting some peace and quiet,' he returned blandly. 'What else?'

CHAPTER FIVE

'THIS is some view,' Jack said. 'But you'd want to have steady feet.'

Hannah followed Jack's gaze into the valley below, where a mist was still rising from the depths of the forest-thick gorge. They were standing on the edge of a rocky outcrop, where the bush track turned sharply before winding its slow route downwards. Less than a metre ahead was a sheer drop, highlighting the dangers of such an untamed terrain.

Hannah had worried about the boys following this track when they'd been younger, and had always accompanied them, pointing out the pitfalls. But, with the passing of years, familiarity had bred a certain amount of contempt. The last time the three of them had been up here for the weekend Chris and Stuart had gone off on their own, and she hadn't felt a moment's concern.

Still, they were sensible boys. Good boys. And not boys for much longer. Chris would be fifteen in November, Stuart fourteen the following January. Her heart turned over as she thought of them. Divorce was always hard on children. At least they had each other, and they genuinely seemed to like their school, which was large on sport and physical activities. Both boys were into sport in a big way.

'You know, I have a definite feeling of *déjà vu*, standing here,' Jack said slowly. 'Yet I've never been in the Blue Mountains, to my knowledge. It's not an area I'd ever choose to build in. As you know, I like fairly level land. Rocky hillsides mean a fortune in site preparation or extra foundations. I've never been up here on holiday either, from what I can recall. You did say you hadn't brought me up here during the last six weeks, didn't you?'

He turned to face her, his question forcing her to look up at him, which was highly unfortunate. She'd been trying not to look at him too much, ever since he'd reappeared in the kitchen for breakfast, dressed as she'd never seen him dressed before.

When she'd gone up to his apartment yesterday, to pack some clothes for him, Hannah had just grabbed an assortment of warm tops and jeans, plus a couple of jackets, choosing neutral colours which wouldn't clash. Cream, white, grey and black. She'd expected Jack to do what he always did—mix and match his clothes pretty haphazardly. She'd never imagined for a moment that he would choose to wear all black.

But he had—probably without realising the effect it would have, or the fantasies it would evoke in Hannah's mind.

When he had strolled back into the kitchen after his shower, his wet hair looking even blacker and longer than usual, his face still unshaven and his tall, macho frame encased entirely in black from head to foot, Hannah's hazel eyes had nearly fallen out of her head. Even the scar on his cheekbone had added to the image he had unconsciously been projecting.

He'd looked wild, and wicked. And she'd wanted him to make love to her. Wildly and wickedly.

The only comfortable thing about that hot memory was that Jack hadn't been looking at her as he'd come into the room, giving her a few seconds to pull herself together before she'd served him his bacon and eggs.

When she looked up at him now, her feelings hadn't changed. She still felt the sexual impact of his bad-boy appearance, but at least she was learning to control those responses, learning not to gape or blush or drool.

Her eyes still travelled over him, however, noting the way the short leather jacket hugged his hips, showing how slim they were compared to the breadth of his chest and shoulders. Her gaze dropped further, to take in the taut curve of his buttocks before travelling down the muscular length of his legs, clearly outlined in his tight black jeans. Swallowing, she swept her eyes back up to his, hoping that she wasn't betraying the way her heart was suddenly thudding heavily in her chest.

It wasn't much comfort to find Jack staring back down at her, though she didn't think it was because he was similarly entranced with her own appearance in faded blue jeans, an ancient red jumper and an equally old dark navy duffle-coat. Her only surrender to femininity had been some red lipstick. Unless one also counted her leaving her hair down—although she'd told herself that that was for warmth, not because she wanted to look younger for Jack.

'Hannah?' he prompted, somewhat brusquely. 'I asked you a question. Have you or have you not brought me up here before?'

'No,' she told him quite truthfully. 'I haven't.'

He frowned, then turned to scowl at the panoramic scene before him, his narrowed gaze scouting the horizon with its unusual bluish haze then sweeping downwards. 'That waterfall seems very familiar,' he said, indicating the small stream of water which was cascading down the cliff opposite before settling in cool grey pools in the rocky creekbed below. 'I'm sure I've seen it before,' he muttered.

Hannah knew exactly what he was remembering without realising it—his recent jaunt up here with Felicia. Hannah hated thinking about his having spent the whole of last weekend in bed with that bitch—though whether her feelings were jealousy or guilt over her own present lustful state, she wasn't sure. She only knew that she wanted Jack herself. It was as simple at that.

'You must have seen hundreds of documentaries about the Blue Mountains on telly over the years,' she attempted to explain, though agitatedly. 'That's what you're probably remembering.'

His sideways glance was sharp. 'No,' he denied, 'it's not, and you know damned well it's not. You're lying to me, Hannah.'

She gasped when he grabbed her nearest shoulder and spun her to face him properly, his other hand taking possession of her other shoulder so that she was virtually imprisoned within twin steely holds. His eyes were just as steely as they darted fury and frustration down at her. 'Tell me the truth, damn it! I *have* been up here before, haven't I? When? Where? Doing what?'

She blushed under the images that sprang to mind. 'Can't you guess?' she threw up at him, her own temper frayed by his touch and his nearness. 'Since it wasn't work which brought you up here, then it had to be the only other thing you enjoy. But you weren't *here*, Jack. You were at a nearby guest-house.'

He frowned, obviously bewildered by her words. 'Why do you keep saying *you*, and not *we*. My God, Hannah, are you saying I was up here with some other woman? Are you accusing me of cheating on you?'

Her silence was both mutinous and wretched. Now she'd done it!

'I don't believe you,' he snapped, letting her shoulders go with an angry twist, then making the mistake of taking a step backwards.

Hannah seemed to see it all happening as though in slow motion, horror rising within her as Jack overbalanced, his arms flailing wildly as he began to fall backwards, into the abyss.

Afterwards she did not know how she'd managed to grab one of those flailing hands, or how she'd stopped Jack's weight from pulling her over that cliff as well. She'd just screamed, then acted impulsively, instinctively, fuelled by a fear-filled burst of adrenalin.

'Jack,' she sobbed, when they both collapsed back on the ground together, a couple of metres from the top of the cliff. 'Oh, Jack.' And she clung to him, weeping and trembling.

'Hush, Hannah. Hush. I'm fine. You're fine. You saved me. Don't cry, now.'

But she couldn't stop crying or trembling, not for ages. They lay there on the ground, arms around each other, their bodies pressed together, Hannah crying and Jack comforting. She didn't really hear the soothing words he said, not after a while. The only physical awareness through the haze of her turbulent emotions was the heat of his body and the beat of his heart against hers. Gradually her shoulders stopped shaking and the tears dried up, and it was then that Jack rolled her over on to her back and kissed her.

She kissed him back.

Dear heaven, how she kissed him back—all the desire which had been building up within her finding full expression in her mouth. Her lips fed on his with avid hunger, her tongue savouring his, first in her own mouth, then in his. Her head lifted from the ground as she strained to make their mouths more as one, a raw, naked moan of need echoing deep in her throat.

Jack's head jerked up; he wrenched his lips away on a ragged gasp.

'God, Hannah,' he moaned, his hands pressing her shoulders back against the cold, hard ground.

She stared up at him, eyes as wide as her wet quivering mouth.

'You can't expect me to stop if we keep this up.'

'I don't want you to stop.'

'You can't mean that. You can't mean me to make love to you here.'

'Why not?' she whispered huskily, her hands reaching up to spear into the hair at his temples, her splayed fingers setting up a slow, erotic massage. 'Don't you want to, Jack?'

'Hell, yes. But I would have thought the boot was on the other foot, if I've been two-timing you.'

'I never said you had. That other business was before we...before we became involved with each other. It doesn't bother me any more,' she lied.

'Yes, but——'

'Just shut up, Jack,' she groaned, 'and kiss me.'

He groaned too, with a type of frustration, but his mouth sank back down on to hers and Hannah shuddered with pleasure. One kiss became two, then three, till neither of them were aware of the hardness of the ground under them, or the coolness of the air around them. Neither of them seemed aware of anything but each other.

Hannah certainly wasn't. She welcomed and answered Jack's increasingly savage kisses with a frenzy of her own. When his marauding mouth slid from hers to graze a hot wet trail across her cheek then downwards, she blindly turned her head to one side, as though offering up more expanse of creamy throat for his ravishment.

And ravish it he did, as wildly and wickedly as she'd been wanting him to. His hands swept her hair aside while his teeth joined his lips in a series of vampirish lovebites which sent the blood pounding through Hannah's veins.

Dazed, she lay there, arms flopped wide on the ground, revelling in the feel of his rough skin scraping over the softness of her throat, gasping at the sharp little nips to her flesh, quivering with pleasure whenever he clamped his mouth down and sucked...hard. A feverish heat swept over her skin, bringing an exquisite sensitivity to the areas on her neck he'd already ravaged and was at that moment ravaging, making them throb with an almost delicious pain.

A shaft of sunlight suddenly landed in Hannah's eyes and she instinctively squeezed them shut against the glare, only to find herself plunged into a world not just of darkness but of blisteringly heightened awareness. To feel, yet not to see, seemed to sharpen her senses. She felt heat gathering between her thighs, felt the swelling of

her breasts under her clothes, felt the growing
urgency of desire as it roared along her veins to
inflame every sexual cell she owned. She was
ready to be made love to as she'd never been
ready before.

Jack must have reached the same pitch of
passion, for suddenly he rolled on top of her,
forcing her legs apart with his, his heavy male
pelvis settling into the gap between her thighs.
When his aroused flesh started pulsing against
the melting valley between her legs Hannah
answered his urging, her own hips lifting from
the ground to grind frantically against him.

Her eyes flew open with a raw gasp when he
wrenched open the waistband of her jeans, then
yanked the zip down. He was kneeling back on
his haunches, dragging at her clothes, his blue
eyes glazed and glittering wildly.

A totally uncontrollable male of Jack's
strength and size was outside of her experience,
and while it seemed frightening at first, to find
herself being stripped so roughly, Hannah
eventually recognised her dry-mouthed, heart-
racing reaction as excitement, not fear. She actually liked seeing Jack out of control this way—
his face flushed with passion, his hands shaking,
his breath coming in harsh, ragged pants.

He swore when he had trouble getting her jeans
and panties over her boots, and in the end he
yanked the boots right off.

Soon, she was naked from the waist down.

By this point Hannah hadn't much control left either. She might have been shocked back to some awareness of cold hard reality if her bare buttocks had been in direct contact with the cold hard ground, but her thigh-length duffle-coat was like a thick blanket under her.

Hannah's only feeling was a fierce impatience to have Jack back on top of her and inside her. Shaking, she sat up to help him take his own jeans down, not waiting for him to do more than ease his clothes down to mid-thigh before she pulled him back down on to her.

'Oh,' she gasped when she felt his naked hardness rub against the swollen lips of her desire. She cried out when he surged inside, stunned by the intensity of pleasure she felt at just being penetrated. She could not wait to have him fill her completely, to feel him move. Grasping his tautly bunched buttocks, she urged him deeper, then deeper, rocking her lower body in a frenzied rhythm.

Hannah was stunned by the speed and strength of her climax. It exploded within her and around him, spasm after violent spasm, quickly propelling him to a climax just as fierce, just as cataclysmic. She gasped at the feel of his flesh pumping powerfully into her, before her lips fell apart on a long, low moan. He muffled that moan by taking savage repossession of her mouth with his, his tongue driving deep, its undulating movements an erotic echo of what was happening inside her.

The Hannah who had brought Jack up here, full of good intentions, was shocked—both by the primitive nature of their mating and the feelings it was evoking in her. She knew, even as the passion began to ebb away, even as Jack's mouth slipped from hers in a sighing exhaustion, that she would never be the same person again.

She'd crossed a line with this raw surrender—abandoning any thought of right and wrong, giving in to the lust which had been building in her overnight, uncaring about anything but Jack's body blended with hers. The remnants of her conscience kept telling her that she should feel guilt and shame.

But she could not. She was too caught up with what had just happened, and the mind-blowing pleasure it had brought her. Her only concern now was Jack getting his memory back. She no longer wanted him to—at least, not for the rest of this weekend. She wanted him to stay in the darkness—with her—to make love to her over and over, to show her some of that incredible stamina Felicia had boasted about.

Already Hannah wanted him again.

Already...

Her face flamed with the admission. She could hardly believe the thoughts that were going through her head. It was as though she'd become a different woman—a wild, wicked, wilful woman, who wanted to experience everything lovemaking had to offer.

Jack levered himself up on to his elbows and stared down at her, as though he too was seeing a different woman. 'Is it always like that with us?' he said, clearly as shaken by the experience as she had been. That thought gave her even more pleasure. In one fell swoop Jack had wiped out all those years of Dwight telling her she had a very low sex-drive, implying that she was somehow... abnormal.

'Not quite,' she said, hardly recognising her own voice. It was low and husky, sleepy and sexy.

'It was... incredible,' he murmured, still looking a little stunned. 'Incredible...'

She reached up to run a fingertip over his lips, and he sucked in a startled breath. 'Are they sore?' she asked dreamily.

'Not as sore as your neck, I'll warrant. Good God, Hannah, I don't know what came over me. You'll be black and blue for days.'

She didn't doubt that. It crossed her mind that she'd never seen any lovebites on Felicia's neck. Which shouldn't have made her feel smug, but did somehow. 'My hair will cover it. Don't worry.'

'Don't *worry*! I didn't even think to use protection, yet I keep some in my wallet all the time. I've never ever not practised safe sex before. It's a religion with me.'

She reached up to cup his anguished face, her smile soothing. 'Jack, darling, I'm on the pill.' Which was just as well, she realised, for she hadn't given much of a thought to such matters either.

'I've been taking it for years,' she went on, 'and when I left Dwight I simply didn't stop. Believe me when I say there's no chance of your becoming a father this weekend. And believe me when I also say there won't be any other unfortunate consequences from our making love without using protection.'

When she lifted her head from the ground and delivered a light little teasing kiss to his mouth, his nostrils flared, his startled eyes showing that he could not get used to such a Hannah as the one he was encountering. Hannah herself wasn't used to this new self of hers either. But she was loving it.

She'd never felt so confident in herself before. Or so rampantly sexual. She just had to kiss him again. Had to *have* him again.

Her hands snaked around his neck and she pulled him down, down on to her mouth and into the darkness once more. He half resisted for a few seconds, but when his flesh started to stir within her he moaned his surrender.

She gathered him in, body and soul, keeping herself half outside the experience at first while she revelled in Jack's rapidly escalating passion, exulted in the power of his surges, thrilled to the tremors that shook him whenever she dug her nails into his buttocks. There was a dizzying intoxication in the knowledge that she could arouse him so, could make him once again lose control.

Inevitably, though, she too was sucked into the whirlpool of need which already had Jack in its tenacious grip. Her heart began to hammer, her head threshed from side to side and her mouth gasped wide, dragging in air to breathe. His name was punched from her lungs, over and over, and when she finally splintered apart under him it was Jack who was ultimately triumphant, Jack who held her sobbing body in his arms afterwards, Jack who gently dressed her and began leading her home.

CHAPTER SIX

'ARE you all right?' he asked softly. 'You haven't said a word since we started back.'

'I'm fine,' she said, though a little shakily. What on earth had happened to her back there? Why had she cried so much afterwards? Why had she felt so shattered when Jack had held her close and comforted her?

'It happens that way sometimes,' Jack said, as though reading her mind and the worries whirling within it. 'We shouldn't have done it again so quickly. Though, damn it all,' he added, a wicked little smile twisting his lips as he looked down at her, 'it was bloody good, wasn't it? When do you think you could manage a third?'

She stared up at him, her mouth going dry at the prospect.

'Come now, Hannah,' Jack reprimanded her softly, taking her in his arms and pulling her hard against his body. 'There's no going backwards now. I always thought your idea of a platonic relationship till I got my memory back pretty silly anyway. We're engaged, woman. We're going to be married. We have every right to make love whenever we want to. Come on, I think a hot shower is called for, and some fresh clothes, then we'll light that living-room fire and snuggle up for the afternoon with some food and each other. What do you say?'

She should have said that no, they weren't engaged. No, they weren't going to be married. No, they had no right to make love whenever they wanted.

But Hannah didn't say any of those things. She was already melting with desire at that last thought, plus the scenario Jack had suggested.

She continued to stare up at him with brightly glistening eyes and slightly parted lips. He groaned, bending to kiss those lips, his arms tightening around her when their tonguetips met.

'God,' he muttered after a minute or two, his hands restless on her back. 'To think I wasted a whole year before I got to know the real you. Let's hurry, darling.'

He took her hand and practically dragged her back up the bush path, eager in his renewed passion. She went with him quite willingly, dazzled by his calling her 'darling', her conscience pushed steadfastly aside.

They had just rounded the last corner which would bring them into the back-yard of the cottage when Jack suddenly ground to a halt.

'What's that?' he asked, pulling Hannah over to one side of the path to stare down at a small brown bundle of fur lying in the long dry grass.

'I don't know,' Hannah said. 'But whatever it is, I don't think it's alive.'

Jack let go Hannah's hand to reach down and touch, moving the bundle carefully. As soon as

Hannah saw the tail uncurl she knew what they were looking at. So did Jack.

'It's a ring-tailed possum,' he said.

'Dead?' Hannah asked, her heart turning over. Nothing moved her so much as the sight of a suffering animal. Better it were dead, she supposed, than mangled.

''Fraid so. She must have fallen out of the tree.'

Hannah glanced up into the branches of the huge overhanging eucalyptus, then back down at the poor dead possum. A branch lay on the ground nearby, one end sprouting forth with freshly jagged splinters, suggesting a recent break.

'Yes,' Jack said, seeing the direction of Hannah's eyes. 'I think she must have been on that branch when it broke.'

'How do you know it's a she?'

'Because there's a baby in her pouch,' he said, and drew out a tiny squirming ball of fur.

'Oh, the poor little darling!' Hannah exclaimed when it began to make frightened little noises, though it quickly quietened after Jack held it under his jacket, clearly finding some comfort in the warmth and darkness. When its head popped back out for a second, Hannah's heart squeezed tight. For it had the cutest little face, with velvety brown eyes, a tiny pink nose and small pointed ears.

'What a sweet little darling it is,' she said, with a wistful sigh.

'Now, don't go thinking you can look after it, Hannah,' he warned. 'Caring for an orphan ring-tailed possum is not the same as bringing up two boys, or even taking a useless bachelor under your wing.'

She blinked up at him. His return expression was wry. 'You do realise you mother me around the office, don't you? You bring in hot muffins every morning, in case I haven't had breakfast. You see all my bills are paid on time. You send out my clothes to the laundry and you even remind me sometimes when I should get a haircut.'

She blushed furiously, feeling oddly hurt by his teasing remarks.

'No, I'm not making fun of you—or complaining, or criticising,' he insisted. 'I *love* being looked after. It's something I never had when I was growing up and I've been selfish enough this past year or so to take advantage of your maternal instinct—although I think you get some pleasure out of doing these things. You're a born mother, Hannah.'

'Do you think that's what I want to do with you?' she snapped, still hurting inside. 'Mother you? I assure you that's the last thing on my mind where you're concerned, Jack.'

'So I've found out this weekend,' came his drily amused reply. 'To my ever eternal appreciation, I might add. And I aim to take full advantage of that in future, too.'

'Do you, now?'

'Yes, as soon as we can deposit little Possie here somewhere safe. Do you know where the closest vet is?'

'No, actually, I don't,' she returned, her voice still sharp. Though she suspected that the sharpness was directed more at herself than at Jack. She could always say no to his making love to her, couldn't she? She could also enlighten him about who was really his fiancée if she was genuinely concerned by the increasing complications of the situation. *That* would put a halt to any lovemaking for a while; that was for sure!

But she already knew that she wouldn't do any of those things. Not today. Today she would let him do whatever he liked with her, whenever he liked, so fierce was her desire for him.

Hannah scooped in then let go a shuddering sigh of total surrender. She neither had the strength nor the will to fight the feelings he kept evoking within her. How could she, when they were all so new and so very, very exciting? She could not remember the last time she'd had a climax while making love, let alone anything like the ones she'd just experienced.

'I do know where we *could* take the possum,' she suggested. 'Probably better than a veterinary hospital, too.'

'Then speak up. Where?'

'There's a lady lives just across the way who often raises orphaned baby animals—especially protected ones like this little fellow. She knows exactly what to feed them and how to look after them. I could take it over myself, if you'd prefer not to come.'

'Why would I do that?' He eyed her warily, no doubt having heard her sigh a moment ago.

She glanced down at his clothes, which were scuffed and dirty from rolling around on the ground. Hers weren't as bad, not being black, nothing a brush-down wouldn't fix. 'You're a bit of a mess,' she said simply.

'You're not much better, Hannah,' he countered drily. 'You might also want to put something around your neck before you go anywhere public. There's one spot which even your hair can't cover. Look, it won't take us a couple of minutes to shower and change. I don't think Possie here will expire in that time, do you?'

Hannah stood in front of the bathroom mirror after her shower, inspecting the damage. It was hard not to feel perturbed with the evidence of their primitive encounter starkly in front of her. Jack had been so right. There was one large purplish bruise at the base of her throat which was impossible to disguise, even with make-up.

She fingered it lightly, wincing and wondering if Jack bore the marks of her nails on his buttocks. The thought excited her. She stared into her own glittering eyes and vowed she would see for herself before this day was out—see and feel and kiss every single spot she'd branded with her passion out on that clifftop.

For the first time in ages she also looked objectively at her naked body, trying to see it with positive eyes and not through Dwight's warped view.

She was surprised and pleased to note that she *had* lost quite a few pounds since leaving Dwight—more than she'd realised. Not that she weighed herself any more. Hannah cringed when she thought of the humiliating way Dwight had used to make her get on the bathroom scales once a week, his comments scathing if she'd put on even half a kilo since the last weighing, his attitude still scornful if she'd only succeeded in maintaining her weight.

It also seemed that going to work had toned her up more than all those aerobic classes Dwight had insisted she attend.

Not that she had always gone. Sometimes she had slipped away to a movie, just to escape into another world for a while. And naturally one couldn't go to the movies without buying a large cup of popcorn plus a chocolate-coated ice-cream, all washed down sweetly with a huge Coke. Later, of course, Hannah had been consumed with guilt, and those had always been the weeks when the scales had told the tale—when Dwight had invariably pinched the beginning of a roll on her hips, his contempt obvious in his face.

She turned sideways and inspected her hips and bottom in the mirror, surprised to encounter not a hint of real flab or cellulite. Her hips *did* flare out from her waist, and her buttocks *were* well-rounded—nothing would ever change her natural body-shape—but enticingly, she thought, if a man liked womanly curves.

Turning back, she was satisfied to note that her stomach was fairly flat as well—only a small swell under her waist, which she didn't think unattractive. She had a nice navel, she thought. A neat little circle, dipping in.

Hannah's eyes lifted from her navel to above her waist, and she frowned. No way would her cup C breasts ever stand out high and perky as they had when she was nineteen. After nursing both her sons they'd settled in lower, heavier curves on her chest. In a push-up bra her bust was still very impressive, with a smashing cleavage if she ever chose to display it, but once the bra was removed the full globes did drop to a more natural outline.

Dwight had castigated her for breast-feeding the boys, saying it had ruined her figure. But she didn't really agree. Surely it was a matter of individual perception and taste? She thought the lusher look suited her womanly body. Nursing had certainly improved the shape and size of her nipples, which had been almost inverted before. Now they were well formed, pointy and highly sensitive. They'd also darkened from a pale rosy colour to a duskier shade of pink.

A banging on the bathroom door brought a gasp from her lips.

'What in hell are you doing in there, Hannah?' Jack called out. 'Get some clothes on and let's go.'

'OK. Won't be a sec. I'm just getting dressed now.'

Flushing, Hannah dived into the clothes she'd picked out for herself while Jack had showered and changed. Rather sexy black underwear, a pair of stone-washed grey jeans, a red polo-neck, which more than adequately covered her neck, and a stylish navy blue blazer-style cardigan with brass buttons.

She slipped her feet into navy loafers, then snatched up her hairbrush.

Despite her heart racing, she took some time to do her hair, parting it carefully and smoothing it down to her shoulders, where she used the circular brush to tease and turn the natural curl under, then spraying it to keep it in place. Full make-up was out of the question, but she stroked a little mascara on her lashes then applied some red lipstick, finishing up with a small spray of Sunflowers perfume. Hannah suspected that she would not get another opportunity for feminine titivating before Jack made love to her again, and she wanted to be at her best for him.

Thinking about Jack making love to her certainly brought colour to her cheeks, so there wasn't any need for blusher. Hannah took one last glance at herself, decided she looked pretty good, swallowed nervously, then exited the bathroom—only to find Jack pacing up and down the hall, talking to the baby possum in his hands and looking absolutely gorgeous in tight faded blue jeans and a huge cream cable-knit sweater.

He ground to a halt at her reappearance, glaring at her as a Viking might have glared at some maiden he was about to ravish.

'Damn, you look good enough to eat,' he muttered, his eyes sweeping over her, then fastening on her scarlet mouth. 'What a time to have to play Florence Nightingale to a possum! Still, I dare say we couldn't relax and enjoy ourselves while this poor little thing went to the big eucalyptus tree in the sky. So, where exactly is this lady's place?' he asked, tucking Possie under his jumper.

'Only about a hundred metres away, actually. We go back up the track I drove down last night for a short distance, then turn right along a small path through thick bush which opens out into a clearing. Marion's house stands right on the back edge of that clearing, overlooking the valley.'

'Is that her name? Marion?'

'Yes. Marion Cooper. She's married and her husband's name is Edward. Oh, and Jack, let's not mention your amnesia.'

'Why in hell would I mention it? We're just going to leave the possum and come straight back, aren't we?'

'Well...er...yes, I suppose so.'

'Let's go, then. The sooner we get there, the sooner we'll get back.'

Hannah hurried after him out of the house, stopping only long enough to lock up and stuff the key back in the geranium pot. She suspected that they might not get back as quickly as Jack anticipated, for Marion was not the sort of woman you dumped a possum on, then swiftly left. Neither was her husband given to letting a visitor get away, however unexpected. In a way, it was going to be interesting to see how Jack handled them both.

CHAPTER SEVEN

'HANNAH!' Marion cried with obvious and abundant pleasure when she opened the front door.

In her mid-fifties, Marion was a very big woman, tall as well as wide, given to wearing voluminous caftans in vivid Hawaiian patterns, regardless of the season. Today, her ankle-length dress had a white background with a red hibiscus print—the same outrageous red as her red frizzy hair.

'How nice of you to come and visit us,' she gushed, bright blue eyes twinkling. 'Edward!' she called back into the house. 'Hannah's here. And she's brought a friend. Light the barbecue, darling, and get out some wine.'

She turned back to face an already flustered Hannah. 'Well, aren't you going to introduce me to this gorgeous man?' she said, staring past Hannah straight at Jack.

Hannah cast a worried glance over her shoulder at Jack, met his drily amused eyes, and relaxed. 'This is Jack Marshall, Marion. My...er...um...'

'Fiancé,' Jack put in solidly before she could decide what to call him.

'*Fiancé*!' Marion exclaimed, looking from Hannah to Jack to Hannah again. 'But you said nothing last weekend about being engaged when we ran into each other down at the shops.' Marion managed to sound mildly aggrieved and absolutely intrigued at the same time.

'It...er...it only happened this last week.'

'Oh, how lovely! I'm so happy for you, dear. I was worried that you might not want to get married again after putting up with that frightful husband of yours for years. But I'm so pleased you are. Life is far too lonely without a partner to share it with. I'd be lost without my Edward.'

She gave Jack the once-over, her expression admiring. 'And haven't you done well for yourself this time! Now, this one is a *real* man, if looks are anything to go by—which of course they aren't, but it's a nice start. Marshall, did you say your surname was?' she rattled on, frowning first at Jack then back at Hannah. 'You work for Marshall Homes nowadays, don't you, dear?

'Yes.' Hannah felt a guilty blush gathering.

Marion's pencilled eyebrows lifted, her blue eyes twinkling some more. 'But how romantic! Now, do come along inside, both of you. It's rather fresh out. Much warmer in the family-room.'

A sideways glance at Jack reassured Hannah that he was resigned to at least a short visit. Marion did rather overwhelm one, but she was such a generous soul underneath that Hannah didn't like to say no to her impromptu invitations.

Hannah had met her soon after Dwight had bought the cottage, succumbing to an on-the-spot invitation to dinner when they'd met down at the local video store. Dwight, however, had never hidden his contempt for a woman who looked and dressed as Marion did, though he had tolerated her company occasionally, in order to drink some of her husband's rare red wines.

'Actually, Marion, we didn't come over to impose ourselves on you,' Hannah elaborated swiftly as they were ushered inside. 'We found a dead ring-tailed possum in the bush this morning, and it had a baby still alive in its pouch. I told Jack you were just the person to look after it.'

'A baby ring-tail!' she cried, clapping her plump hands together in a gesture of prayerful gratitude. 'Oh, I just *adore* baby ring-tails! Where is the poor little darling? You have brought it with you, haven't you?'

Jack lifted his jumper and extracted his furry passenger, Marion's face just melting as he put the curled up ball into her motherly arms. 'We've called him Possie,' he said, surprising Hannah with the catch in his voice. It seemed that the little possum's plight had managed to spark an emotional response in the macho man by her side, evoking his protective instinct—or perhaps even his paternal instinct?

'Don't you worry, pet,' Marion reassured him—the 'pet' aimed at a startled Jack, not the possum. 'I'll look after your Possie. Ah, there you are, Edward. Take our guests down to the

family-room, will you? And get them a drink.
I'll whisk this little sweetie out into the kitchen
and fix him up with a bed and a bottle. Yes, it
is a him,' she added after a quick look. 'Oh, and
by the way, Edward,' she threw over her shoulder
as she waddled off, 'Hannah and Jack are engaged. He's Jack Marshall of Marshall Homes.
Hannah's boss. Don't you think that's
romantic?'

Edward said that it was, shaking his head as
his wife went off, clucking and cooing over her
new baby.

In his early sixties, he was as lean as Marion
was wide. A very tall, aesthetically elegant man,
he had silver-grey hair, a stylish silver beard, and
a strong Roman nose separating intelligent grey
eyes. Dressed in dark grey trousers, a polo-necked
blue pullover and a tweedy jacket with leather
patches on the elbows, he looked like a country
squire or the conductor of a symphony or-
chestra. He was, in fact, a retired public servant
who had a passion for all things fine—music,
books, wine. And his wife.

He was Marion's second husband, her first
having divorced her when she was twenty-five
after they'd found out she couldn't have children.
Crushed, she'd turned to food for comfort over
the next twenty years, and had been a staggering
two hundred kilos when she'd met Edward in a
doctor's waiting-room. He had been a widower
at the time, with a grown family.

They'd clicked immediately, and under Edward's encouragement Marion had trimmed down to a much healthier one hundred kilos, at which point he'd told her that he liked her as she was, and that if she didn't want to diet any further it was all right by him. Ten years after their marriage they were still inseparable, living up here in their mountain hideaway.

'You do realise that I'm going to be seriously neglected for at least a week,' Edward said drily as he led them into the gloriously spacious family-room which Hannah had always admired.

It stretched across the back of the house, floor-to-ceiling windows giving an unimpeded view of the mountains in the distance and sliding glass doors leading out on to a wide wooden deck which overlooked the valley below. Facing north, the room was pleasantly warmed by the winter sun—Edward only having to light the open stone fireplace on overcast days.

A long benchlike table stretched under the middle window, bathed in sunlight but littered with books and magazines of all sorts. Edward scooped up the magazines and dumped them in the nearest corner, just missing a large Persian cat which was stretched out, sleeping in a pool of sunlight. It didn't even flinch, showing that it was used to Edward's haphazard method of tidying up.

'Choose a chair,' he directed. 'If you can find an empty one.' In truth, most were occupied by other feline creatures of various breeds—all of them reluctant to give up their favourite spots. Jack managed to find a free seat, but Hannah ended up sharing hers with an overweight Abyssinian.

'You've more cats than ever, Edward,' Hannah remarked.

'True,' Edward said resignedly. 'Marion can't resist them. She likes having animals around her, but after all the demands her native orphans put on her she needs her own pets to be of the independent type. When she finally comes in here to relax, she doesn't want any animal needing anything more from her than one feed a day and the odd stroke.'

'Why does she do it?' Jack asked. 'Raise native orphans, that is.'

'It satisfies her maternal instinct,' Edward said. 'Marion can't have children, you see. Didn't Hannah tell you?'

'Er... no, she didn't.'

'Sad thing, not being able to have children.'

'I wouldn't know,' Jack said rather stiffly. 'I've never wanted to have any myself.'

'Really? Why's that?'

Jack shrugged, but underneath the seemingly nonchalant gesture Hannah detected a degree of discomfort. This was clearly something he didn't like talking about. 'I guess I don't see myself as good father material at this late stage,' he muttered. 'I'll be thirty-five next birthday.'

'Positively ancient,' Edward chuckled drily. 'So what shall I get for us to drink, Hannah? A nice

Hunter Hermitage to go with our steaks, I think. And some tawny port for afterwards. Have you any preferences, Jack?'

When Jack hesitated before answering Edward looked perplexed. 'You *are* staying for lunch, aren't you? I've already started up the gas barbecue outside.'

'Of course they're staying,' Marion said as she bustled in, carrying Possie in what looked like a tiny Christmas stocking made out of a satin-edged blanket. His little mouth was clamped on to a miniature bottle, sucking madly, and his tiny paws clasped around it much like any other baby. 'A nice Hermitage will be perfect! Here, Jack, you finish giving Possie his bottle while Hannah helps me make some salad.'

'*Me!*' Jack sat bolt-upright, looking aghast.

'Why not? You'll want to get your hand in at feeding babies if you're going to marry Hannah. If I know her, she'll want some more sons—or maybe even a daughter.'

Edward cleared his throat. 'Er…Marion, love, Jack says he doesn't want children.'

Marion flashed Jack a look which one would have given to an escaped serial killer. But then she laughed. 'Don't be ridiculous, Edward. Everyone *wants* children. If Jack says he doesn't it's probably because there's something wrong with him. Maybe he has some sort of congenital defect which he doesn't want to pass on—isn't that right, Jack?'

Hannah's heart turned over with sympathy for Marion. The woman's deep pain at not being able to have children had never been more obvious. She simply could not accept that anyone would choose not to have them.

Hannah caught Jack's eye across the table, silently pleading with him to be gentle with the obviously distraught woman. He nodded almost imperceptibly, then looked up at their tensely waiting hostess. 'You're quite right, Marion,' he said gently. 'I do have a problem which I would not want to pass on to any children of mine. How very astute of you to realise that.'

He sent Hannah an odd look, and it crossed her mind that maybe he wasn't lying. Maybe he *did* have something wrong with him. He certainly was very emphatic about not having children. She stared thoughtfully back at him, but before she could glean the truth from his face he turned his eyes back to Marion, who was now bathing him in the full force of her own sympathy.

'Oh, dear. You poor man. But we must not dwell on what we cannot change, must we? We simply have to get on with our lives and do what we can. Which includes looking after poor little mites like this fellow, who can't look after himself. So here...' She thrust the bundle and bottle into Jack's startled arms. 'Have a taste of second-hand fatherhood! You might find you like it.'

Hannah watched, totally intrigued, while Jack's face went from frightened to fascinated to downright infatuated within no time at all. He couldn't seem to take his eyes off the baby possum as it gleefully sucked on the bottle, at the same time appearing to stare adoringly up into the man's face above. I know you, those soft brown eyes seemed to say. You saved me. You're my hero. I love you.

Tears welled up into Hannah's eyes and she had to turn away, a choking emotion filling her heart and her throat. It was a silly, typically feminine reaction to sentimental thoughts, but she could not help it, and it embarrassed her. Hoping no one was noticing, she looked down and blinked madly, surreptitiously wiping the corners of her eyes and not looking up again till she felt in better control.

But when she did, Marion was staring straight at her with a puzzled expression. Hannah somehow found what she hoped was a disarming smile and stood up. 'You did say you wanted me to help you with some salad, didn't you, Marion?'

'I certainly did. And you, Edward,' she ordered, 'down to the wine cellar!'

Hannah thought she'd successfully side-tracked Marion from any awkward questions, but no sooner had she begun cutting up the assortment of vegetables Marion placed on the chopping-board than the inquisition began—and it was an inquisition, despite it being couched in more tactful terminology then earlier on.

'Jack's a very good-looking man,' she said carefully. 'And I'm sure he's a wonderful lover. But do you think marriage is a wise course, Hannah? Your divorce has only just come through, hasn't it?'

Hannah swallowed, then decided not to take this conversation too seriously. It wasn't as though she was really going to marry Jack. 'Don't worry, I won't be rushing into the actual wedding, Marion. I'm aware this...er...relationship could be a bit of a rebound reaction. But it's very nice having a man treat you the way Jack treats me.'

'He's kind, is he?'

A warm feeling washed through Hannah. 'Oh, yes...he's very kind.'

'That's good. I hope you don't mind my saying so, but Dwight was an out and out pig of a man. The way he put you down in front of us used to make me seethe. If he hadn't stopped coming up here with you when he did, I would have stopped inviting you over—simply because I could not bear to see you so unhappy. I don't know how you stood it for so long.'

Hannah's sigh carried a wealth of remembered misery. 'I don't know how I did either. But he...he had such a domineering personality, Marion. When I first met him I thought he was wonderful. I actually admired his intelligence and ambition. Once I married him, though, I began to see his flaws. There was a meanness about his inbuilt arrogance—a desire to belittle others to make himself feel even better and smarter. I, being his wife, was the perfect target. I was his whipping boy, and, because I thought I loved him, I allowed myself to be whipped.'

'You're not saying he beat you, are you?'

'No. He was never abusive. Not physically. But there are all kinds of abuse, Marion. I've only recently come to realise that he abused me mentally and emotionally. His constant complaints and criticisms robbed me of all my self-respect and self-esteem, whittling away at it over the years till I really believed I was fat and stupid and undesirable.'

'Fat!' Marion's eyes bulged with shock. 'And stupid? And undesirable? *You?*'

'Yes, I know,' Hannah said with a sad sigh. 'That's how sick in the head he made me. Towards the end, I believed everything he told me.'

Marion was shaking her head. 'Dear heaven, that's terrible. And was he critical of the boys as well?'

'Would you believe me if I said no? They could do no wrong. But there again, he probably saw them as being in his own image and likeness. They do look very much like Dwight, you know, though actually they're not at all like him in nature. They're physical rather than intellectual boys. Thank the Lord they're pretty smart too, so he hasn't noticed yet.'

'You have joint custody, don't you?'

'Yes. To give Dwight credit, he hasn't been vindictive about the boys. Of course, by the time I left him he'd been about to leave me anyway, having found his perfect spouse.'

'Perfect in what way?'

'Oh, physically. And sexually too, I guess. Naturally I never did measure up in that department either. He was giving his new choice a final audition in his surgery one day when I walked in on them. Oddly enough, my reaction was a cold anger—not shock. Underneath, I'd known for ages he was having affairs. But seeing it for myself seemed to fill me with the courage to change my life. Luckily the boys were in school, so I moved out that day and a month later started working for Jack as his secretary. He...he——'

Hannah broke off, a prickle of awareness at the back of her neck making her turn her head and look over to the doorway which led back into the family room. Jack was standing there, staring at her. How long he'd been standing there or how much he'd overheard, she had no idea. His blue eyes gave nothing away, remaining cool and unreadable.

Marion looked around and saw Jack too. 'He's finished the bottle, has he?' she said, putting down her knife and walking over to him. 'How did it go?'

Jack's face broke into a smile. 'Great. He's a greedy little beggar. Didn't leave a drop.'

'That's good. I'll just take him out and hang him up in the laundry.'

Jack looked taken aback. 'Hang him up? What do you mean?'

'I have an assortment of pegs on the walls, where I hang all kinds of beds for all kinds of babies who are used to being in trees. They seem to like the arrangement. Come with me and I'll show you. Be back in a sec, Hannah. Just keep chopping.'

Hannah kept chopping, hoping that Jack hadn't heard too much. She didn't think that he had. Maybe just the last little bit, about her walking in on Dwight and Delvene. He already knew about that anyway. She'd told him herself. But her earlier very brief recounting of her marriage and its break-up had not revealed the depth of Dwight's domination over her person and personality.

It was one thing to tell Marion she'd allowed herself to be bullied and humiliated by her husband for years, quite another for Jack to know about her belittlement and abasement. The only way she wanted Jack to look at her was with admiration and desire—never pity or, dear God, disgust.

Still, it had felt good to tell a sympathetic ear what a swine her husband had been. Perhaps it was something she should have done months ago, but she'd been too ashamed, believing that she should not have put up with such degrading treatment for so long.

Hannah could see now that one of the reasons she had was because she had had no family support, no one close she could go to for help and advice. She was an only child, and her mother had died many years before, when Hannah had been just fifteen. Her father had insisted she leave school shortly afterwards and do a secretarial course, so that she could earn money and help support his gambling habit. He had been a cold, unloving man, and she'd felt no guilt whatsoever over leaving the family home as soon as she'd secured a decent paying job which would support her.

When her father had turned up at her office one day and made a big scene, she'd been asked to leave, so Hannah had moved further, from Wollongong up to Sydney, getting a job at Sydney University as secretary to one of the professors at the Faculty of Medicine. She'd met Dwight there, when he had come to the university one day as a guest lecturer on plastic surgery. He'd been twenty-nine to her nineteen. He'd asked her out and been astounded when she wouldn't sleep with him on their first date. Or their second. Or their tenth.

He'd married her three months later—Hannah still a virgin.

Looking back, she could appreciate now that their wedding-night had proved a big disappointment to him—she'd cried all night from the pain of their first encounter, not letting him near her again. Things had improved the next night, but clearly she had never fulfilled the sexual fantasies that had propelled him into marrying a girl who'd obviously been too young and too shy for him.

In fact, she doubted that Dwight's sexual infatuation had lasted much longer than it had taken her to get pregnant. Since their first son, Chris, had been born exactly nine months and one week after their wedding-day, the writing had been on the wall from the word go.

Hannah's mulling over her marriage was interrupted by Jack and Marion returning, arm in arm, both commenting smugly over Possie's progress. Apparently, after Marion had attended to the animal's toiletry needs with some tissues, the little devil had curled up in his pretend pouch and gone straight to sleep.

'What a good baby he is,' Jack told Hannah proudly. 'A right little trouper!'

Marion chuckled. 'Give him a couple of hours and he'll be whingeing out there with the best of them. Still, that gives us time to feed our own faces and have a nice long chat. I wonder what *vin extraordinaire* Edward has selected for our delectation this afternoon?'

'Actually, Marion, I'm just a beer man myself,' Jack informed his hostess, and she laughed.

'Not for long, dear man. I don't know anyone Edward hasn't corrupted to the sort of grape he serves. But I'll make a deal with you. Have one glass, and if you don't like it I'll bring you some beer. Fair enough?'

Jack had more than one glass. He had more than one bottle! A grandfather clock was chiming five by the time they left Marion and Edward's place—Jack having insisted that they stay, not just for one but for two more possum-feeds.

'Come back and visit again tomorrow!' Marion offered as they left, to which Jack happily agreed.

'You really liked them, didn't you?' Hannah said as they made their way back down the bush track, the setting sun throwing deep shadows across their path. 'It's not just the possum.'

'Why so surprised, Hannah?' His arm stole around her shoulders and he pulled her close, reminding her forcibly of where they'd been before they'd found the baby possum and gone to the Coopers' place five hours earlier.

'Most people find Marion a little...er...pushy.'

'Most people, Hannah? Or just that unfeeling sadistic bastard you were married to?'

Hannah's eyes dropped to the ground. 'Oh...so you did overhear.'

He turned her to face him, but she kept her eyes lowered, feeling mortified.

'Look at me, Hannah.'

She did—slowly, unhappily. 'What?'

'I'm not going to ask you about him. Or your marriage. I heard quite enough. I'm just going to tell you that I find you beautiful, and clever, and quite, quite wonderful. I meant it the other night when I said you were more woman than any I would ever have thought to possess. I'm crazy about you, Hannah. When are you going to marry me?'

CHAPTER EIGHT

HANNAH'S hesitation frustrated him.

'Don't come out with that "wait till you get your memory back first" crap,' he growled. 'Can't you see I'll never get those six weeks back? They're gone, Hannah. Whoosh! And who cares? I can remember the most important part— my sexy secretary and hopefully soon-to-be wife.'

Hannah blinked up at him. 'You really find me sexy, Jack?'

'Distractingly. I always thought you extremely desirable, but I was deceived by your ladylike manner into thinking you were somehow above sex for sex's sake. I used to watch you at work and wonder if you ever looked at a man—yours truly included—and really fancied him in the most basic way.

'I used to fantasise about being alone with you in the office—late at night—and suddenly those lovely hazel eyes of yours would start looking me over with such a raw, naked need that I would be instantly hard. I won't tell you the rest of my fantasy or you'll think me very crude. Suffice it to say I can well imagine how I reacted at finding you in my arms that night in the office.'

'What night?' For a split-second Hannah had forgotten about the story she'd told Jack concerning the way they'd first become physically involved. 'Oh, yes. That...that...night. I...er...I don't like talking about that when you can't remember it.'

'Not to worry. I'm having fun making new memories of what we're like together. If this morning is anything to go by I can't wait for more. Still, I think a more leisurely session is called for, don't you?'

He snaked his hands around her waist under her cardigan, then down over her bejeaned buttocks, caressing and kneading them with strong, knowing fingers. When he pulled her close, moulding her stomach around his starkly aroused flesh, her heart kicked over violently and her eyes widened on his.

'I'm going to take you home, light that fire in the living-room and make love to you,' he said thickly. 'Every time you waver from the idea of being my wife I aim to make love to you. If necessary, I'll make love to you all night. You're going to say yes to me in ways you haven't even thought of yet,' he vowed darkly. 'And when morning comes, you're going to say yes to me in the only way that matters. You're going to say yes to our marriage, once and for all!'

Hannah stared up at him, totally speechless as he swung her up into his arms and started carrying her back towards the house. By the time he made it up the front steps on to the porch some small measure of conscience had kicked back into her brain, and she tried to say something. But it was then that he kissed her, firmly dispensing with any scruples.

'The door's locked,' she whispered when he lifted his mouth from hers to try the doorknob. 'Lean me down to that geranium pot and I'll get the key.'

'Bloody stupid place for a key,' he muttered.

'Yes,' she agreed dazedly. She would have agreed to anything at that moment. 'Shall I put it in for you?'

'Don't be provocative,' he growled, and she blushed fiercely. 'But, yes, you'd better. I've got my arms full.'

'You're very strong,' she said as he carried her inside and kicked the door shut behind them.

'Having a physical profession does have some pluses, I guess.'

Her hands slid over his chest, feeling its power beneath his jumper. 'You have a great body, Jack.' What she'd seen of it, that was. Presently she aimed to see a whole lot more. And touch a whole lot more.

'It's all yours, love,' he said as he angled her through the living-room doorway. 'Hell, but it's freezing in here. Do you think we should give this room a miss, put on the electric blanket and dive into bed?'

Hannah looked rather glazedly up into his glittering blue eyes, happy to go along with whatever he wanted.

'No,' he went on, before she could say a thing. 'I don't fancy that at all. Since I can't remember

if I've brought my office fantasy about you to
life, we're going to live out the one that played
through my mind last night, on that sofa over
there. Correction. On those *two* sofas over there.
I take it you've no objections?' he asked, his
mouth dropping to brush seductive lips over hers.

'Whatever you want, Jack,' she agreed huskily,
the blood beginning to pound a sensuous beat in
her temples.

'You shouldn't make such broad-sweeping
promises,' he said, and lowered her back on to
shaky feet. She swayed and he caught her to him,
their eyes locking, their mutual passion pulsating
through the air around them. 'I just might take
you at your word.'

For several exquisitely tense moments she
thought he was going to strip her and take her
on the sofa then and there. But eventually he let
out a ragged sigh and put her from him, a wry
smile twisting his mouth. 'Patience, Jack,' he
muttered to himself. 'All good things come to
those who wait. Show me where to get the wood,
Hannah. I have no intention of spoiling a whole
evening of potential pleasure for a few seconds
of instant gratification.'

The next half an hour was the most excruciating half-hour of Hannah's life. They both
went about the task of making the house warm
and comfy for the approaching night—collecting
a good supply of wood then lighting and building
up both fires, first in the living-room and then
in the kitchen.

Neither looked at each other much, underlining the sexual tension gripping both of them, but the delay—plus Jack's obvious intention of making love for hours in the living-room and not in a bed—had resurrected several of Hannah's old doubts about her figure-faults. She hoped he wouldn't be disappointed in her body. She hoped he wouldn't be disappointed in *her*.

This morning, out in the bush, had been entirely different. They hadn't even taken off all their clothes, their mating being more of the 'wham-bam thank you, ma'am' variety.

Not that she'd minded. It had been what she'd wanted. What they'd both wanted. Technique hadn't come into it. It had all been raw, primitive passion, with no thought of who should do what, where, or for how long. What Jack called a more leisurely lovemaking session, however, evoked all sorts of misgivings and inadequacies in Hannah.

Dusk came while they were busy with the fire in the kitchen.

When Hannah left Jack there to walk back down the hall to check the living-room fire, she found the room very dim, with only the glow from the now roaring fire throwing off any light. She automatically reached up to turn on the switch just inside the doorway, crying out with fright when Jack's hand suddenly covered her hand, removing it from the switch. Her eyes flew to his, puzzled, reproachful of his frightening her like that.

'That kind of light is not in my fantasy,' he explained softly, lifting her hand to his lips and sipping at each fingertip in turn.

Hannah stared at him, transfixed when he started sucking her middle finger into his mouth, only an inch at first, then deeper... deeper...

'I... I thought only women had fantasies,' she choked out.

He withdrew her finger, his chuckle like dark velvet. 'Don't you believe it. I suspect, however, that a man's fantasies are a little more starkly sexual than a woman's.'

'And don't *you* believe *that*,' she whispered, hazel eyes heavy as her finger moved to seek re-entry.

She saw the flare of surprise in his own eyes, but then they narrowed and darkened as he sucked her finger back into his mouth, watching her all the while.

Hannah was in a daze of desire, her heart thudding behind her ribs, her stomach curling over. God but she actually wanted to do that to him—and not just to his finger either. She wanted to do a whole lot of things she'd never wanted before.

Heat bloomed up into her face at this admission. Or was it a confession? Dwight had insisted she do all sorts of things she hadn't really wanted to do, and of course, because she'd loved her husband—or believed she had—she'd complied. But she hadn't been at all comfortable with a lot of his demands, her feelings ranging from embarrassment to revulsion to fear that she would not do them right.

She had always been afraid of any activities which she might not perform to Dwight's perfectionist standards—such as herself being on top. On the few occasions she'd done *that*, in the early years of their marriage, Hannah had felt humiliated by Dwight's instructing her all the time she'd been doing it—telling her which muscles to squeeze, how far to lift her body before lowering it, when to lean down so that he could suck her nipples at the same time.

It had been impossible to find pleasure with his lecturing and criticising her all the time. She'd also frozen during other positions which she'd felt Dwight had demanded in order to humiliate her, to make her feel subjective to him.

But now...

A tremor quivered through her as she began to see the whole spectrum of lovemaking very differently. Doing things right didn't seem to come into it. Neither did thoughts of humiliation, or of demeaning positions. She wanted to do them all—mindlessly, madly. Jack had been right in saying that she would say yes to him in ways she had never thought of yet.

She would.

Did he know that she would? came the shaky thought. Could he see the abandonment in her eyes, the wanton willingness?

Perhaps. Probably. She really didn't care. She didn't care about anything any more, except Jack making love to her.

'Jack,' she murmured without thinking.

'Mmm?'

'Make love to me.'

His dark brows arched slightly before settling back into their normal beetling position, his hooded eyes the colour of the night in the dimly lit room. He took her finger from his mouth, slowly curling its wet length under, then enfolding her whole hand in his while he led her over in front of the fire.

'Stay there,' he said, placing her so that her back was towards the heat. 'There's something I have to do first.'

Hannah watched, intrigued, while he moved the nearby furniture with quick, decisive movements, lifting the coffee-table and side-tables out of the way, then pushing the matching sofas together to form a large bed with sides.

'Won't be a sec,' he said, striding from the room, only to return less than a minute later with the quilt and pillows from the brass bed. When he spread the quilt across the sofa-bed base, tucking in all the sides and smoothing it out, Hannah realised that he wasn't planning on bringing anything to cover them. They were to lie in there naked.

Once again, her confidence was momentarily undermined, till she glanced around the room and realised how flattering the light was. Her stretchmarks—even the little ones on her breasts—would hardly be visible in the warm golden glow of the fire. Everything, in fact, would look softer and younger and better.

'There!' Jack announced smugly, straightening to stand at the far end of the sofa-bed, glancing around the room. 'Have I forgotten anything? Ah, yes, the door. Can't let any of this delicious heat out.' And he moved over to close it, turning afterwards to face her across the room, his back against the door.

He was well outside the circle of light which radiated from the fire, so she could not make out the expression on his face. Or his face at all, for that matter. But she saw his arms cross over to grip the bottom of his cream jumper, saw him tug the garment up over his head and toss it aside.

He stood there, naked to the waist but still in shadow. She could just make out the impressive proportions of his shoulders and torso, but not much else.

'Take off your cardigan,' he ordered from the darkness, his voice low and fuzzy.

She hesitated, then did as he asked, her hands shaking.

'Drop it on the floor.'

She did.

'Now the sweater.'

It fell in a red pile on top of the cardigan, leaving her standing there with only a skimpy black lace bra between herself and nudity from the waist up. Her heart was pounding in her chest, her mouth drying as she wondered whether he would ask her to remove that as well.

'The bra too,' he husked, and the breath hissed between her teeth.

'No!' he counter-commanded, when her hands stretched shakily up behind her to undo the clasp. 'No...'

He came towards her then, breaking into the light, revealing a chest as magnificent and primitive-looking as she'd imagined. The colour of teak, it was covered by a fine matting of dark hair which thickened into a rug of black curls at the centre of his powerful chest muscles. His arms bulged with equally powerful muscles, throwing into contrast his washboard stomach and slender waist. Hannah ached to run her hands over him, to splay her fingers into those curls, to trace over the steely curves of his arms, kissing the path of her fingers as she went.

'Let me,' he said thickly once he reached her.

Hannah shivered when his hands slid up her bare arms, sucking in a strangled breath when he slipped the bra straps off her shoulders, letting them dangle at her elbows. Without their support, her full breasts settled lower, and the lacy half-cups only just covered her nipples.

She swallowed when he started tracing a lazy fingertip down over the swell of one breast, dipping into the chasm of her cleavage before climbing the other curve, bypassing her throbbing nipple by a mere millimetre. She swallowed again when he returned to the straps and peeled them down further, holding her breath as the cups gave up their secrets, gasping when she felt her nipples spring naked and stunningly erect before his eyes.

She searched his face for any sign that he thought them in any way disappointing, but found nothing but an avid and passionate concentration. He began to touch them, making her tremble. When he bent to lick them her eyes closed on a quivering sigh of ecstasy.

Hannah was beyond minding when he finally removed her bra, knowing nothing but a rapidly escalating desire to lie totally naked with him, to have his mouth and hands on all those other places which were burning for him. As he tossed aside her bra she was already kicking off her shoes, her hands busy on the zipper of her jeans. He saw her haste and matched it with his own, stripping off the rest of his clothes just as quickly.

Within seconds they were both naked, both panting. Hannah's eyes swept over him and she couldn't help thinking that he certainly was twice the man Dwight was—in more ways than one.

'Don't look at me like that,' he growled. 'You're embarrassing me.'

Startled, she glanced up at him. She had never thought of a man like Jack as ever feeling embarrassed. 'But you're so beautiful,' she said earnestly.

'Some women don't like big men.'

'Then they're fools,' she whispered, placing both her hands on his chest and sliding them slowly downwards. She felt him tremble when she passed his ribs but she would not—could not—stop. She had to touch him, had to show him how beautiful she found him.

He shuddered under the caress of her hands, sucking in repeated ragged breaths when she continued to touch him with long, stroking, loving movements.

'Enough,' he barked at last, and swept her up into his arms. 'You can do as much of that as you like later,' he ground out. 'But for now this is *my* fantasy. *My* turn to do the touching. Agreed?'

'Yes, Jack,' she agreed. 'I want whatever you want.'

'You might live to regret those words.'

'I might live to regret a lot of things,' she said, knowing the truth of it. 'But never you, Jack, and never tonight. Tonight I am yours to command. Tonight I will do whatever you want.'

'You mean that?' he husked.

'Yes.'

'God, Hannah. God...'

She woke to find him lying on his side, facing her and watching her with heavy, sated eyes. Smiling sleepily, she rolled over towards him, tipping up her chin in search of his mouth. He bent his head slightly, sipping briefly at her lips, reminding her how sensitive they were.

Which was only to be expected, she thought, her stomach curling over as the memories flooded in. But not with shame. She would never feel shame with Jack. Everything they'd done together was beautiful and natural. Everything *she'd* done had been done with desire and affection and total willingness.

Never in her life had she ever felt so beautiful and sexy as she had tonight. Jack had not been able to get enough of her attentions, allowing her free rein over his magnificent body for as long as she wanted.

And Felicia had been so right, the bitch. He did have a quite incredible stamina—not only was he able to last a long time once he put his mind to it, but he was quick to arousal again, even after the most torrid climax. She gained the impression that he would have been quite happy to go all night, bringing to life every single fantasy a man could have, but it had been she who had finally succumbed to exhaustion, drifting into a deep and dreamless sleep.

'What time is it?' she asked, her voice sounding drugged.

'Does it matter?'

'Not really.'

'I put some more logs on the fire,' he said. 'It was going out.'

She levered herself up on to an elbow, pushing her hair out of her face at the same time. There was no self-consciousness about her nudity any longer. Jack loved her body. He'd told her so often and at such length that she finally believed him.

'Have you had any sleep?' she asked him.

'Some.'

'I need to go to the bathroom,' she said, and scrambled out over the back of the sofa nearest the fire.

'Don't be long.'

'I won't.' She leant back over the lower arm-rest end and dropped a light kiss on his mouth. 'Don't go away,' she whispered into his lips.

His large arms lifted up over her head, cupping the back of her head and pressing her mouth back down. His mouth opened wide under hers, inviting her to send her tongue down inside. She did, and his lips closed around it, sucking hard. Desire flooded back into her veins and she moaned softly. By the time he let her go, she almost stumbled from the room.

The bathroom mirror was cruel with its vivid reflection of her ravished state. The bruises on her throat had faded somewhat, but there were new ones on her breasts and her thighs. Hannah stared at them, fingered them lightly, but still could not feel shame.

She'd loved every minute. There was no point in denying it. She also loved the woman she'd become tonight, with Jack. No more feelings of inadequacy for her in bed. No more sick-making nerves. No more imagining herself sexually inferior to other women—women like Felicia.

Hannah flinched. She wished she'd stop thinking about *her*. It reminded her of the problems to come, when Jack got his memory back. Even if he didn't get his memory back there would still be problems. If she didn't tell him herself about his real fiancée, people at work would. No doubt, sooner or later, the wretched woman herself would turn up, demanding answers.

No, she would have to tell Jack herself.

Tomorrow. In the morning. Over breakfast.

But that was still several hours of darkness away—several hours in which she could lose herself in a world she'd only just discovered, a world full of bittersweet pleasures which she suspected only Jack could give her.

She picked up the hairbrush lying on the vanity unit and began to put some order into her tangled hair. Afterwards she cleaned her teeth, rubbed some soothing salve into her lips, sprayed some eau de cologne over her whole body and then, taking a deep gathering breath, whirled and left the room.

CHAPTER NINE

'THERE'S something I've been meaning to do,' Jack said as soon as she climbed back into the sofa-bed and lay down beside him.

Hannah's heart fluttered when he picked up her left hand; she was not sure what he was about to do.

'I don't want to see these on your hand again,' he muttered, wriggling her wedding and engagement rings off her finger and dropping them into her palm. 'That wasn't a marriage you had. That was torture. Give them away,' he said sharply. 'Or sell them. Or put them in a deep dark drawer, if you like. As long as I never have to see them on you again.'

Hannah blinked her amazement. Jack acting proprietorial about her was an even newer experience than having him as her lover. Lifting her eyebrows slightly, she knelt up, reached over the high curved back of the sofa, and dropped the rings carefully on to the carpet. She stayed kneeling there for a few seconds, leaning her elbows along the top, staring blankly into the glowing fire and trying to work out if Jack's attitude pleased or annoyed her. Finally she glanced over her shoulder at him, only to find him frowning at her as though he too was not happy with the way he'd just acted.

'You're not going to marry me, are you, Hannah?' he said, in a low, taut voice.

She could not bring herself to lie. 'No, Jack,' she replied evenly. 'I'm not. And please don't ask me why.'

An emotion she could not identify choked her throat then, and she looked away, feeling utterly bereft. It totally confused her, for it didn't seem to have anything to do with guilt, but despair. His materialising behind her, gentle hands on her shoulders, tender lips on her neck, only seemed to make it worse.

'Don't, Jack,' she choked out. 'That won't work. I'm not going to change my mind.'

'Hush, my darling,' he murmured. 'Hush.'

'No, don't,' she groaned when he started tracing her spine with kisses, his hands trailing down with him, brushing past the edges of her breasts, which were pressed flat against the sofa-back.

'You don't understand,' she cried softly, then shivered violently. His lips and hands had reached her buttocks and weren't stopping.

'It's all right,' he murmured between kisses. 'I understand. It's too soon...much too soon... We'll just be lovers for now...and not think about anything else.'

She moaned at these words, for indeed she couldn't think of anything else—not when he started easing her thighs apart.

I must not surrender to this again, came the whirling feverish thought. Must not. I'm losing control of my life again. Losing control...

He stopped. Just in time, she thought shakily.

But any respite was to be brief. She tensed when she felt his body slide into the valley between her legs. She ached for his possession, yet feared it at the same time. There would be no control for her then. None.

He delayed the inevitable, however, tormenting her by rubbing himself slowly back and forth over her desire-slick flesh, making her quiver whenever he contacted nerve-endings already sensitive from their earlier lovemaking. Her whole body tightened when his huge frame loomed up behind her, enveloping her totally.

His hair-roughened chest pressed against her back, the stubble on his chin grazing her soft skin as he rubbed it over her shoulder. It felt as if she was being covered by a wild animal in the jungle, the thought making her mouth go dry with excitement. She felt utterly helpless, pinioned as she was against the sofa, Jack's huge muscle-hard body wrapped around hers. Still, her very helplessness held a perverse pleasure—the pleasure of total abandonment and surrender to Jack's superior male strength and size.

A sob caught in her throat, for while she was incredibly turned on she did not want to feel like this, did not want to allow any man this type of dominion over her. She tried to push back away from the sofa, but he misinterpreted her movements as the urgency of passion.

'Soon, darling, soon,' he murmured thickly.

She whimpered with dismay when he pressed her back even harder against her sofa, raining rough kisses over her shoulders and neck. He stroked her hair aside with shaking hands, moving his lips up her throat to nibble at her earlobe.

'Beautiful Hannah,' he breathed into her ear, then ran his tonguetip around it. 'Beautiful sexy Hannah.'

Her buttocks clenched tight as a shiver of erotic delight ran down her spine. He stroked her hair back some more, winding it through his fingers then turning her face so that he could cup her chin and kiss her properly. Her pitch of excitement flared wildly when his tongue surged hungrily into her mouth. Quite unconsciously she began pulsing her lower abdomen back and forth against him.

He groaned and abandoned her mouth, moving one hand down to splay it wide against the soft swell of her stomach, then pressing her back so that her body arched into his. She felt herself being lifted, and whimpered at the desertion of his body from between her legs till she realised what he was going to do.

She tensed, gasped, then groaned. Slowly he lowered her back on to her knees, the action making his penetration complete. She shuddered violently, not wanting him to move, yet at the same time wanting it quite desperately.

'You are one incredible woman,' he rasped into her hair. 'Tell me you'll never stop being my lover. *Promise* me.'

'I promise,' she said, then shuddered again as he began to move.

'I'll never let you go back on that promise,' he warned darkly. 'Never.'

Hannah didn't care, for by then she had ceased to think at all.

'We have to talk, Jack,' Hannah said over morning coffee, although it was almost afternoon. The clock on the wall said twenty to twelve.

They were sitting on opposite sides of the kitchen table, both a little bleary-eyed, both looking as if they might have been at an orgy all night. Jack still hadn't bothered to shave, though he had showered and dragged on the jeans and jumper he'd discarded last night. Hannah had bathed at length, then felt too limp to dress, throwing her pink dressing-gown over her rosy-hued nakedness.

Jack glanced up from his coffee, his blue eyes hardening with an instant wariness. 'I don't see why. I thought we settled everything last night.'

'There...there are things you don't know,' she said tautly. 'Things that happened during those six weeks. Things I...I haven't told you, but should have.'

Jack lowered his mug slowly to the table, every muscle in his face tightening. 'What kind of things?'

Hannah's stomach began to churn. God, but this was difficult. Yet it had to be done. She'd already waited too long.

Her mind raced back to the night before and she shivered. Much much too long, she decided ruefully.

She could not blame Jack. He'd acted like any modern virile man would have with such a willing partner. But she should not have let things go as far as they had. Frankly, in the cold light of day it was hard to believe that the woman who'd inhabited Jack's fantasy bed last night had been herself. She'd had no idea she'd be capable of such wanton behaviour.

Still, she'd gone into everything with her eyes well and truly open. But Jack... Jack had been under a lot of false impressions. He would never have done what he had if he'd known about Felicia. As rotten as Hannah thought the woman was, she was his fiancée, and Jack clearly had felt enough for her to ask her to marry him.

'There *was* an engagement during those six weeks,' she went on, having to practically force the words from her throat. 'And it *was* yours. But it... it wasn't to me.'

A deep dismay swept through Hannah at the look on Jack's face. She had never seen him look so sickeningly shocked. 'Not to you,' he repeated blankly.

'No.' God, but she felt awful!

He simply stared at her, clearly unable to say another word.

'It... it was to a woman named Felicia. Felicia Fay. She's an actress. You only met her recently. It was rather a whirlwind courtship. She... she has blonde hair.'

'Blonde hair,' he repeated, frowning.

His blue eyes slowly widened with a dawning recognition. Clearly he was putting two and two together. The blonde in his flashes had been his real fiancée.

'That party you sort of remembered,' Hannah went on quickly. 'It was actually your engagement party to Felicia.'

'I see,' he said, so calmly that Hannah was startled. She stared at him, not at all sure how to take his reaction. Why wasn't he furious with her? Why wasn't he ranting and raving?

'Might I ask why you pretended to be my fiancée, Hannah?' he said, his eyes narrowed upon her. 'Why you connived to get me up here with you... alone? You must have had a reason.'

'I... I did it on the spur of the moment,' she admitted.

'That much is obvious,' came Jack's dry remark. 'But why?'

'I... I found out something about Felicia at your engagement party—something pretty damning. And I just couldn't bear... I mean, I just couldn't bear... I mean, I just couldn't stand by and see you married to such a woman.'

He stared at her long and hard for several seconds. 'And what was it you found out?'

Hannah frowned. Jack was acting rather oddly, she thought. Not nearly as shocked and rattled as he should be. Either that, or his male pride was forcing him to put on a good act. Well, his male pride was just about to get another serious blow.

'She... she was having an affair with Gerald Boynton. She was only marrying you because Gerald wouldn't and she wanted a rich husband.'

Jack's eyebrows lifted ceilingwards in an attitude of almost mocking boredom. 'Charming,' he said drily. 'And how, pray tell, did you discover these little titbits of information?'

'I'd snuck out on to the balcony for a cigarette during the party,' she explained. 'When I heard the glass doors slide open unexpectedly I thought it might be you, so I hid.'

'As well you might,' came his rueful remark. 'Smoking is a filthy habit. And it'll kill you in the end. Might I remind you, Hannah, that you haven't had a single cigarette this weekend since Friday night?'

Hannah's hazel eyes blinked wide. Had Jack gone mad? What kind of comments were those to make at a time like this?

'Go on,' he said, almost sounding smug.

Totally thrown, she took a few seconds to collect her thoughts. 'I... Well, it turned out to be Felicia and Gerald. At first I thought it was you, because of what they seemed to be doing, but then I re——'

'What, exactly, were they doing?' he interrupted, his tone amazingly bland. Still, she supposed it was difficult for him to feel upset about a fiancée he couldn't even remember.

'They were . . . Felicia was . . . I . . . I'm not sure what they doing, exactly,' she finished, her face flaming.

'Yes, you are. Tell me. There's no need to feel embarrassment, Hannah. There are no sexual inhibitions between us any more, are there?'

Hannah dropped her eyes, not wanting to see any mockery in his eyes. 'She was . . . touching him,' she said, reluctantly and unhappily.

'I presume you mean masturbating him. And what did she say, exactly? Tell me everything. And please, don't spare my feelings. I'll survive.'

Hannah's eyes slowly lifted, but there was nothing in Jack's face to hurt or humiliate her. 'She . . . she said she was only marrying you for your money. She . . . she said you were perfect for her because you were a workaholic and you didn't want children. She did also say that you satisfied her in bed and that you . . . you had incredible stamina.'

One of his dark brows arched sardonically. 'Damned by faint praise. So is that why you pretended to be my fiancée, Hannah, instead of just telling me the truth up front? Because you wanted to sample that stamina for yourself? Not that I'm complaining, mind. It's been a weekend I'll remember for a long, long time.'

She shot to her feet. 'How can you be so cruel?' she said, hot tears stinging her eyes. 'You know that's not true. I was afraid what lies that two-timing slut might tell you about me to make *me* seem the liar. I thought if I got you away alone somewhere, without her influence, I'd be able to make you see the truth. I thought you'd get your memory back within a day or two, but you didn't, and you just wouldn't leave me alone, damn you! I tried to resist. Tried damned hard. But in the end, I just...I just...'

'Just what?' he snapped.

She glared back at him, her lips pressed mutinously together. Surely he could appreciate what he'd done? Surely he had to take some of the blame?

'Go on, Hannah,' he prodded mercilessly. 'Tell me the truth for once. Tell me exactly why you couldn't resist me—why you were so stunningly co-operative last night. What's your excuse? Are you going to put it down to a build-up of frustration? Or have I been wrong about you all this time? Maybe you've become a right raver since you left your dear hubby. Maybe you've been bonking everything in trousers behind my back.'

'You know that's not true!' she cried, hurt beyond belief. 'I'd never been to bed with any man but my husband before you! I certainly had no plans for seduction when I brought you up here. All I wanted was to stop you making the same mistake I did in marrying the wrong sort of person. You took me totally by surprise when you kissed me last Friday night, then capped it all off by saying you'd always fancied me. My own feelings took me by surprise as well. I . . . I'd never thought of you like that before, but suddenly I couldn't seem to *stop* thinking about making love with you.'

'Is that so?' he drawled.

'Yes, that's so!' she lashed out. 'And it was all your fault. You wouldn't stop talking about it! And you wouldn't stop kissing me, damn you. And then . . . when it finally did happen, it was just so incredible. I'd never experienced anything like it before and I simply had to have more. That's the bitter truth of it! Believe me when I say that if you're surprised then I'm shocked to the core. But I'm not going to say I regret it. Neither am I going to say I don't still want you. Because I do. God help me . . . I do!'

Suddenly she slumped down into her chair, burying her face in her hands and bursting into noisy tears.

It was at that precise moment that there came a loud knocking at the front door, followed by a loud male voice. 'Open up, Hannah!' it demanded. 'We know you're in there. Your car's outside.'

CHAPTER TEN

HANNAH's head jerked up off the table, her tears abruptly choked off by shock. Round eyes flew to Jack's equally startled face. 'Oh, my God!' she exclaimed. 'It's Dwight!'

'Yes, but who does he mean by "we"?' Jack scowled. 'Surely he hasn't brought the boys with him, has he?'

'I wouldn't think so,' she said, though shakily. 'This isn't one of the weekends they're allowed home. He must mean Delvene.'

'That bimbo he threw you over for?'

'Yes,' she said tautly. 'That's her name.'

'Good.' Jack's face set into a grimly determined expression. 'I'll enjoy having a word with those two.' And, spinning on the heels of his boots, he stalked off down the hallway.

Hannah scrambled up from the chair and raced after him, grabbing his arm just before he reached the door. 'Wait!' she said. 'Let me see who it is first. It might not be Delvene.' And she pressed her face up against one of the stained-glass panels by the door. A small border of clear glass gave one eye a narrow view. 'Oh, my God,' Hannah gasped, catapulting back as if she'd received an electric shock.

Simultaneously Dwight started banging on the door again. 'If you don't open this door in ten seconds, Hannah,' he snarled, 'we're coming in.'

Hannah threw Jack a stricken look. 'It's not Delvene. It's Felicia. But what on earth is she doing with Dwight? Oh, God, I should have guessed she wouldn't take that fax at face value,' she muttered agitatedly. 'I'll bet she went to the office. They must have told her about your accident, and then the hospital would have told her I said I was your fiancée.'

'What fax?' Jack asked, blue eyes piercing.

Hannah grimaced. There was little point in not confessing all now, but she did so hate the way he was looking at her—as though he would never have believed her capable of such duplicity and deception. She wasn't at all sure if he'd believed her heated outburst of a minute ago, with all its claims of totally innocent intentions. She wouldn't blame him if he didn't. She'd made a right mess of things.

'I...er...I sent Felicia a fax last Friday saying you were having second thoughts about your engagement and were going away for a few days to think it over. I...er...forged your name on it.'

'Hell, you thought of everything, didn't you?' He almost sounded admiring.

'Obviously not,' Hannah returned ruefully. 'I didn't anticipate Felicia seeking out Dwight and making him bring her here.'

'Let me see this Felicia person,' Jack said impatiently, and bent to peer through the glass panels.

Hannah's inner panic turned to instant jealousy. For she knew what he was seeing. Five feet ten of female perfection, dressed casually but eye-catchingly in black leggings, high-heeled black Granny boots and a thigh-length woollen tunic in vivid orange with a black woollen fringe around the bottom. Her long honey-blonde curls were tumbling all over her slender shoulders in sensual disarray.

Jack snapped upright, as though he too had received a shock, which of course he had. His forehead was creased in a dark frown for several interminable seconds. Hannah could guess what he was thinking.

I'm engaged to *that*? I've been going to bed with *that*? I'm supposed to throw *that* over because of one little indiscretion? Hell, what's an affair or two between friends? I only want sex from a woman after all...

Hannah could not believe the dismay she felt at this line of thinking. She could not bear to think of Jack ever touching that woman again. Or any other woman, for that matter. Which was a rather disturbing train of thought. Was her sexual infatuation with him deepening into something more? Or was she just protecting her newly discovered source of physical pleasure?

Whatever, she had to say something—anything to stop him from being swayed by that evil bitch.

'Jack,' she began, 'I know she's very beautiful, but truly she——'

'Don't say another word,' he snapped. 'Not a single solitary word.' And, taking her hand firmly in his, he wrenched open the door just as Dwight was about to knock again.

Hannah had never before seen her ex-husband look so much at a disadvantage. His hand remained frozen in mid-air for a second, his elegantly handsome face not quite so elegantly handsome with his mouth and eyes doing a good imitation of a goldfish. His disbelieving gaze swept first over Jack's rugged masculinity before moving down to Hannah, who could feel her cheeks going as pink as her dressing-gown and slippers.

'*See*?' Felicia squawked from beside him. 'What did I tell you? Your precious ex-wife has not only been pretending to be *my* fiancé's fiancée, but she's been living the part as well! Just look at her! If that isn't a woman who's wallowed in bed with a man for the last two days then I don't know what is! My God, I'll warrant she hasn't got a stitch on underneath that robe. If I know Jack, I'll bet she hasn't had a stitch on since they arrived.'

Hannah felt Dwight's stunned grey eyes travel over her again, slowly this time, taking in all the signs of the tempestuous weekend she'd spent with Jack. In vain, she clutched the lapels of the dressing-gown together. For *nothing* could hide the marks on her throat, or the bruised state of her lips.

'My God,' was all he could say, each word a shocked whisper.

Felicia schooled her face into an expression of earnest anguish, then took a step towards Jack, placing a tentative but caressing hand on his free arm.

'Jack, darling, don't you remember me? It's Felicia, honey, your *real* fiancée. We met at Gerald's place. You must remember Gerald.'

When Jack remained stonily silent, Felicia sent Dwight an anguished glance. 'You see? I told you he had no memory of me. I knew that fax wasn't from him. *She* sent it, that conniving bitch there, who always tries to look like butter wouldn't melt in her mouth.' She dropped her act for a second to let her natural viciousness blaze through, her mouth looking quite ugly under a nasty sneer till she rallied and regrouped her skills for another tender assault on Jack.

'When you had your little accident and lost your memory of me, darling, that despicable woman there told the hospital *she* was engaged to you, but she's not. *I* am. You've been cruelly tricked, darling. Cruelly and maliciously. She always hated me and she always wanted you. I could tell from the first moment we met. She used to be nice to me in front of you, but when you were out of earshot she was sour and mean. God knows how she thought she could get away with it, though. The mind boggles!'

Hannah wanted to cry. Dear heaven, but she was convincing, even managing to squeeze a tear from those large limpid blue eyes of hers. As for her luscious coral-painted lips . . . They trembled with feigned emotion so beautifully that Hannah would not have blamed Jack if he'd believed her.

'God knows how *you* think you can get away with *this*, Felicia,' he said, each word so cold and biting it froze the blonde on the spot.

It rather froze Hannah as well. Good Lord, if she hadn't known better, it would have sounded as if he had his memory back!

But of course he hadn't, she quickly reasoned, so he had to be acting. Still, it seemed he'd decided whom he believed in this situation, and Hannah's heart swelled with emotion. She moved her fingers within Jack's hand and he squeezed them tight, the reassuring gesture almost bringing tears to her eyes.

'*Jack*!' Felicia finally recovered, to protest— the perfect picture of injured innocence. 'My God, whatever has she told you about me?' she cried brokenly before turning on Hannah. 'Oh, how could you be so wicked?'

It was surprisingly easy, Hannah thought, a small smile tugging at her mouth. And compared to you, darling, I'm a saint!

'If I wasn't seeing this with my own eyes,' Dwight said, shaking his head and combing his perfectly groomed fair hair back from his frowning forehead with perfectly manicured hands, 'then I wouldn't belive it.'

'Wouldn't believe *what*?' Jack ground out, his anger hitting Dwight like a physical blow, for he took a step backwards. 'That the beautiful woman you married and did your best to destroy would ever have the courage to seek comfort in another man's arms?'

Hannah's hazel eyes blinked wide up at Jack. She was thrilled by his words, and his defence of her actions—thrilled and flattered and quite overwhelmed.

'I can understand your not believing it, you unspeakable bastard,' Jack raged on, splendid in his championship. 'You did your best to crush her confidence in herself as a woman, to make her think she wasn't desirable any more. But I'm here to announce you failed!'

Hannah gazed adoringly at her lover, then with dignified contempt over at Dwight, who was looking grey and sick.

'Yes, Hannah and I have been making love,' Jack went on, his voice loud and proud. 'We've been making love all damned weekend. And it's been so bloody fantastic I know I won't ever *stop* wanting to make love to her!

'As for *you* . . .' he swung back to face Felicia, who was looking pretty ashen-faced herself. 'I asked you before, now I'm asking you again. How on earth did you think you were going to get away with this?'

'With what, Jack?'

'Coming up here and playing the devoted and wronged fiancée. The last time I saw you, on Thursday night, you were scrabbling in the gutter, trying to get your engagement ring out of the drain—the ring you threw at me after I told you the wedding was off!'

Felicia paled some more, if that was possible. Hannah found it hard even to think. So Jack *did* have his memory back. But since when? And what was he talking about? He'd actually called his engagement off, back on the night of the party?

'You…you've got your memory back,' Felicia said, obviously shaken to the core.

'Yes. I remembered everything soon after Hannah walked into my hospital room.'

Now it was Hannah who was shaken to the core, till Jack's tightening fingers made her see that he was lying. He *had* regained his memory, but not when he was saying he had. It had probably happened some time after Felicia and Dwight's arrival.

'It was *my* idea for Hannah to say she was my fiancée,' he continued curtly, 'simply to facilitate getting out of that damned hospital. Some fool had mistakenly mentioned I had one, and I didn't want to explain anything to the doctors and nurses. I just wanted to get out of there. The doctors insisted I go somewhere quiet for a few days because they were worried about concussion. I remembered Hannah's cottage up here and asked her if she would bring me here for the weekend.'

Hannah swallowed, and tried not to look guilty. Lord, but he could lie well. Almost as well as she had found she could this weekend.

'Hannah hasn't been pretending to be my fiancée since we left the hospital,' came his next clanger. 'If you think she tricked me in some way to seduce me then you're quite wrong. If there's been any seduction around here this weekend it has been all on my part.'

Well, that bit was pretty right, Hannah thought wryly.

'I've always been attracted to Hannah, and once I had her alone, and away from the office, I decided to act on that attraction.'

'But... but what about that fax I received?' Felicia argued desperately. 'If it was really you who sent it—and it must have been if you had your memory back last Friday—then you said you were reconsidering our engagement...'

Hannah's stomach contracted. Who would have believed that what she'd thought was an outrageous lie could have been interpreted this way—that Jack had been thinking about re-instating his engagement, not breaking it!

'Jack,' Felicia said softly, in the most engagingly pleading tone. 'Look, I know you were upset on Thursday night about me and Gerald, but our affair really *was* over by then—believe me. I hadn't been with Gerald since meeting you. We weren't doing anything in the bathroom together, truly. I was simply telling Gerald it was over.'

Hannah was beginning to get the picture. Later that evening—no doubt after she'd left to go home—Jack had caught Gerald and Felicia in some kind of compromising position together, and had successfully put one and one together to make a disgusting pair!

Jack was arching a cynical eyebrow at his ex-fiancée. 'Somehow I doubt that, Felicia. I think perhaps you were finishing what you started out on the balcony earlier that evening. Don't bother to deny it. There was a witness out there who has subsequently told me what you and Gerald were up to. So you can forget about that fax. Our engagement is definitely off, believe me.'

'What witness?' she demanded to know, her face all red and blotchy with anger. 'Oh, I see. It was Mama Bear here again, this time sneaking around and spying on me, then lying her head off to make me look bad.'

Jack's laugh was harsh. 'No one has to make you look bad, Felicia. You *are* bad. In fact, you're rotten through and through, and so is Gerald. Now, get out of here, and when you get back to Sydney don't forget to ring your sleaze-bag lover and let him know what he can do with his deals. I don't want to ever see either of you again!'

That was the straw that broke Felicia's back. She went white. For a split-second she looked as if she might collapse, but, true to her true nature, she soon recovered, all pretence gone from her face. Her blue eyes were vicious as they raked over Jack and then Hannah.

'So you've won, bitch,' she snarled. 'I hope you're happy with your prize. He's not such a catch, you know. Oh, he has plenty of money, and a certain macho appeal, but I have a feeling that won't be enough for you, Mama Bear. You'll always want the whole romantic deal, won't you? Plus the patter of little feet. He'll never give you that, honey. Never!'

Whirling away, she walked with cold arrogance back down the steps, head held high as she strode over to get into the passenger side of Dwight's new BMW. A blue one this time, Hannah thought blankly, trying not to let Felicia's barbs hurt her.

But they did hurt. Horribly. She hardly dared look at why too closely. She kept telling herself valiantly that she didn't want any of those things from Jack anyway. She'd only just divorced Dwight. The last thing she wanted was another marriage and more babies.

As for Jack's love... She'd long known that Jack wasn't the type of man to fall in love. Oh, yes, he could like, admire and desire a woman. But love? He hadn't been given any as a child, and she didn't think he knew what it entailed.

'Why don't you go too?' Jack suggested caustically to Dwight, once Felicia had slammed the car door. 'Take the woman back to where I last saw her. It's where she belongs.'

Dwight, who had recovered some composure by this point in time, gave Jack a hard look, then turned slightly softer eyes to Hannah. 'I know you won't believe me when I say I'm sorry,' he said, in an astonishingly regretful tone, 'but I am. I had no idea. I guess I never have had much idea about other people's feelings. Dad's always telling me Mum spoilt me rotten—giving me far too much attention, filling me with all sorts of notions about what I could become and what I deserved out of life.'

Hannah could appreciate that. She'd never got along with her mother-in-law, who had made it perfectly plain from the word go that she thought Hannah not good enough for her one and only son. Oddly enough, however, she liked Delvene even less. Maybe Dwight would never pick a woman his mother would approve of.

'I told myself I was trying to help you, but I can see now how much I must have hurt you...'

Hannah was stunned by his seemingly sincere words.

'I hope you'll find it in your heart to forgive me. I love our boys, and I think they would like their parents to be friends. What do you say?'

When he extended his hand she simply stared at it, unable to think or to move. Dwight apologising was far too alien to her concept of his personality. She kept looking for the hidden putdown, waiting for the emotional slap in the face.

'The man's been man enough to say sorry, Hannah,' Jack said softly by her side. 'Be woman enough to at least accept his apology.'

When she remained frozen to the spot, Jack took her lifeless right hand and placed it in her ex-husband's. She stared down at his fingers closing around hers and thought of the time when they'd first met, and something as simple as his holding her hand had made her heart sing.

But her heart stayed silent this time. Silent and sad.

It was over, she realised. Over.

The hurt and the humiliation were gone—forever.

Now her heart did move, and her eyes began to swim. She looked through blurring lashes, first into her ex-husband's face and then up into Jack's, wanting to tell him that he'd been responsible for the cure but unable to find the words.

'I think you should go,' Jack told Dwight curtly. 'She's been through enough for one day.'

Dwight nodded slowly. Letting Hannah's hand go, he stretched out a hand to Jack. After an initial hesitation, Jack took it.

'Look after her,' Dwight said.

'I will.'

'She's a fine woman.'

'The finest.'

'You don't know what you've damned well got till you've lost it,' he muttered.

'Worse after you've driven it away,' Jack reminded him.

'Yes.' Dwight scooped in then let out a shuddering sigh. 'But there's no going back. I'm still the same man anyway. I can't change.'

'We can all change,' Jack told him. 'It's never too late.'

Dwight flashed Hannah a thoughtful look, and she wondered if he was thinking how changed *she* was.

And she was.

She would never again let a man make her decisions for her—never let anyone else convince her that she was less than she was. She might not be perfect, but she was as good as anyone else and better than most.

'Goodbye,' Dwight said with a weary sigh.

When he moved to turn away, something propelled Hannah forward. She clasped his arm and reached up to give him a kiss on the cheek. His returning look was so bleak that her eyes filled with tears again.

'Does that mean you forgive me?' he rasped.

She couldn't say so out loud; she just gave him another kiss on the cheek and ran inside. She was leaning against the wall sobbing when Jack came in and took her in his arms. He held her head against the wall of his chest, stroking her hair with one hand and her back with the other.

'You really loved him, didn't you?' he murmured.

'I...I suppose so,' she choked out. 'But I was...only a child...when I married him...'

He sighed, the action filling his huge lungs before expelling the air slowly. 'Well, you're not a child any longer, Hannah. You're an adult woman. So dry your eyes and tell me what you want of me.'

His abrupt question had the effect of definitely drying up her tears, her hands reaching up to dash them from her cheeks as she looked up at him. 'What...what do you mean?'

'I mean, Hannah, do you want to make your pretence a reality?'

'You mean, you...you still want to marry me?'

'Yes, I do.'

'But we don't love each other,' she protested, despite feeling a small twinge of guilt at this statement. Maybe she did love him. Maybe she was simply hoping to urge him into saying he loved her. She was certainly holding her breath to hear his answer.

But his reply wasn't what she wanted to hear at all.

'You were in love with Dwight,' he growled, 'and where did that get you?'

'It wasn't my loving Dwight that was at fault, Jack. It was the fact that he didn't love me back. You need to both love each other.'

He glared at her, his face grim, his eyes frustrated. 'So your answer is no.'

'It has to be, Jack.' God, but why did she feel so wretched? She was doing the right thing, using her head for once. Because of course she wasn't in love with him. She hadn't been last Friday, and what had happened to change that? It was the sex confusing her. She'd gone a little sex-mad for the moment.

'I hope you don't think we can go back to things as they were before,' he said brusquely. 'I couldn't bear to work with you without having you as my lover as well. You must know that.'

'Yes, I know that,' she admitted, knowing it all too well. She knew she couldn't go back either. 'I want you as much as you want me, Jack.'

He pulled her to him, his arms steely with suppressed anger. 'I suppose I should have known you wouldn't fall in love with a man like me,' he bit out.

'Jack, I——'

'Shut up, Hannah,' he snapped. 'Just shut up.'

And he kissed her—furiously, hungrily.

When he started dragging the dressing-gown off her shoulders Hannah placed her palms on his chest and pushed back, wrenching her mouth away from his.

'Have...have you forgotten we promised to visit Possie today?' she said shakily, fearing that she was only seconds away from being successfully seduced again. She just couldn't let Jack ride rough-shod over her body all the time, or Lord knew where things would end up

'Is this your way of telling me you don't want to make love right now?' he sighed.

'Not really. I'm merely delaying things—that's all. We have all the time in the world, Jack. You...you could stay the night at my place tonight, if you like.'

'You mean, we're not staying here?'

'Not if you want us to get to work on time in the morning. I also hate driving down the mountains in the dark, so I thought we'd leave around four.'

'But it's already after one!'

'Then we'd better hurry along and see your little possum friend, don't you think?'

Fifteen minutes later they were locking the front door, Hannah having pulled on the jeans and pink jumper she'd worn on the Friday night then done a quick make-up and hairdo, twisting her hair into a loose knot on top of her head. They had just set off up the bush track, walking hand in hand, when a sudden thought crossed Hannah's mind and she turned to face Jack.

'Oh, I forgot to ask you. When *did* you get your memory back? I know it wasn't last Friday, like you said. If you say it was before last night I'm going to kill you.'

He looked down at her with a wry smile on his face. 'The truth is, Hannah...I haven't.'

CHAPTER ELEVEN

HANNAH'S mouth flapped open. 'You *haven't*?'

'Nope.'

'But . . . but . . .'

'I had a couple of those flashes, that's all. Remember when I peeped through the front door at Felicia? That's when it happened.'

Yes, she remembered. She'd thought he'd been shocked by her beauty, and had been thinking how desirable Felicia was, making Hannah herself feel awful.

'In one flash she was taking a ring off her finger and throwing it at me,' he went on. 'Then I saw her down on her hands and knees in the gutter, looking for it. That's all I remembered. I simply improvised. I said what I knew, hoping she'd hang herself. And she did.'

'Then you still can't really remember her? Either your meeting or your romance?' Hannah didn't want to admit how thrilled she was that he didn't. He couldn't very well compare them in bed if he didn't even remember the woman.

'I can't see myself having a *real* romance with a woman like that. Oh, she's good-looking enough—and, brother, can she put on a good act. I dare say she got me in with an abundant supply of sex and flattery. I've always been a bit of a sucker for that from a beautiful woman, I must admit.'

'The sex or the flattery?' Hannah said drily.

'Both.' He wound steely arms around her waist and curved her body to his. 'Like to try some on me, beautiful lady?' he murmured.

'Don't be silly,' she said, but a little too breathlessly to be convincing. He'd just delivered some flattery of his own, calling her a beautiful lady. Hannah knew that she was equally susceptible to flattery—maybe even more so. And she was very susceptible to Jack holding her.

'I hope you're not going to carry on like this in public,' she warned.

'Like what?'

'You know. Grabbing me all the time. There's no need to, you know. You've already got me where you want me.'

'And where's that?' he asked, his blue eyes intense as they moved over her face before settling on her mouth.

Wanting you all the time, she thought, with a measure of self-exasperation.

But Hannah could hardly say that, so she searched for a suitably flip retort to defuse the sexual tension again building within her. 'In your private and personal office, of course,' she quipped.

He scowled, her answer obviously not pleasing him. 'Oh, I aim to have you there, Hannah. And any other place I can corner you. I told you I'd never let you go as my lover and I meant that.'

He glared at her, his jaw squaring stubbornly, his eyes a steely blue. Hannah began to worry that she'd merely exchanged one ruthless man for another.

Thank God she hadn't allowed him to bulldoze her into a hasty marriage. She had a suspicion, however, that he hadn't given up on the idea.

'I think we should get along to Marion's, don't you?' she said, proud of her firm tone. She certainly wasn't the same weak ninny who'd married Dwight. She would cling to that thought every time Jack put the hard word on her, in more ways than one. 'Time marches on.'

'*Dead*?' Jack repeated, his face and voice suggesting that he wasn't familiar with the word. 'Possie's *dead*?'

They were standing in Marion's kitchen, both of them stunned by Marion's bad news.

Jack's shock quickly gave way to a frustrated anger. 'But he *can't* be dead!' he raged. 'He was just fine yesterday. You said so yourself.'

Marion's kind round face showed true sympathy. 'I know,' she murmured. 'But it happens like that sometimes. No matter what you do, during the first twenty-four hours they sometimes start to pine for their mother and they just die. When he stopped drinking during the night I knew he was in big trouble. He was very young, you know.'

'You should have come and got me,' Jack said accusingly. 'He seemed to like me. I might have been able to do something!'

Hannah saw the hurt in Marion's eyes and placed a soothing yet warning hand on Jack's arm. 'It wouldn't have made any difference, Jack,' she said gently. 'Marion's obviously seen this happen many times. She did her best. You did *your* best. You have to let it go. It's nature's way. Possie's mother died when he was too young to survive.'

He fell silent then—painfully, broodingly silent. But finally he rallied, a deep shuddering sigh racking his big frame. 'Yes, of course. You're right,' he said bleakly. 'I'm sorry, Marion. I shouldn't have taken it out on you. He was just such a cute little beggar.'

'Babies have that effect on you,' Marion said, her eyes teary.

Her sadness moved Hannah, and she stepped forward and gave her a big comforting hug. 'There'll be plenty more baby possums for you to look after, Marion. And others. You do a grand job looking after them. Now, where's Edward? Jack and I have to go back to Sydney soon, but I don't like to leave you like this, if you're all alone.'

'No, he's here somewhere. Down the back, I think, looking after his herb garden. You mean, you can't stay a while?' she gave Hannah such a pleading look that Hannah knew she couldn't refuse.

'Perhaps for a cup of coffee.'

'Oh, that's lovely. Edward will be so pleased. He was looking forward to seeing you again today, Jack. He did so enjoy your company yesterday. I'll put the kettle on and go and find him.'

Hannah turned to face Jack rather reluctantly once Marion had bustled off. He was as silent and grim as she'd feared, but there wasn't any criticism over her agreeing to stay for coffee. He didn't even seem to see her staring at him, his mind off in another world.

'Jack? Are you all right?'

Visibly shaking himself, he focused on her and smiled. But it was not a happy smile. It was just a surface politeness, or maybe even a cover for some deep inner pain. She had a feeling he'd been thinking about something that went way back— maybe something from his childhood. But she knew he wasn't about to tell her, even if she asked him.

Men like Jack never talked about themselves—not on any deeply personal level. They thought such confidences weakened them, or made them look less than the strong macho image they presented to the world.

Hannah found such an attitude sad, for it meant that basically they remained lonely souls, never confiding their innermost feelings to each other.

Not that Hannah could judge him too harshly. She'd never been one of those women who could tell another woman anything and everything.

Maybe this was the result of her mother dying young, or having no brothers and sisters. She wasn't sure, but she'd kept herself to herself on the whole. She'd never had a best girlfriend—not even in her schooldays.

How many times had she overheard the girls who worked in the various offices at Marshall Homes telling each other their life stories over a cup of tea, envying their openness, plus their ability to laugh at themselves and their relationships?

She decided then and there to be a little more open herself in future—not to hug her hurts to herself. No doubt such insular behaviour only made one's problems seem worse than they perhaps were. She wondered even now if she'd exaggerated the things Dwight had done in her mind, getting some of them way out of all proportion. Maybe he hadn't been deliberately cruel, merely totally insensitive.

Difficult, however, to become an instant communicator when Jack was standing there, arms aggressively folded, obviously in the grip of a black depression.

'I could do with a cigarette,' she announced, hoping that might snap him out of his mood.

'What? Not bloody likely!' he growled. 'And if you think you're going to smoke while you've got me captive in that car during the drive back to Sydney, then you can think again!'

'I can see you've put your "boss" hat back on,' she quipped, sliding an arm through the crook of Jack's elbow and dazzling him with a saucy smile. 'Or is this your "protective lover" hat?'

He frowned down at her. 'What are you up to?'

'Up to?' She feigned innocence—almost as well as Felicia, she thought. For with her touching Jack she was already projecting ahead to tonight, the thought of having him with her in bed all night making her quiver inside. How exciting to be able to roll over at any time during the night and fondle his incredible body, arouse it with her hands or her mouth...

She coloured a little when she found Jack's narrowed eyes on her face, knowing that her thoughts had betrayed her.

'What on earth are you thinking about, woman?'

She knew she was blushing, but she refused to feel ashamed. 'You want the truth, or a white lie?'

'Which one will get me what I want?'

'Are we still talking about marriage, or sex?'

'Oh, I've given up the idea of marriage,' he practically snarled. 'A man has to appreciate when he's hitting his head up against a brick wall. I'll settle for the sex, Hannah. The kind that had you blushing a moment ago.'

Hannah blushed some more, a type of shame now joining a perverse hurt over Jack's no longer wanting to marry her. She should have been relieved. Instead she felt upset, and rather confused. She no longer knew what she wanted any more.

'I . . . I wasn't thinking about sex,' she lied, her eyes dropping from his.

'Yeah, right,' he drawled. 'So if I told you I wouldn't be staying with you tonight, what would you say?'

Her eyes snapped up, her bewilderment laced with anger. 'Is this your way of punishing me for not marrying you?'

'Not exactly. What if I suggested you come to my place tonight instead?'

'No,' she refused.

'Why not?'

'For one thing I don't want any of the staff catching me coming downstairs from your apartment in the morning,' she said, quite truthfully.

'You think it'll look better my arriving in the passenger seat of your car?'

'Probably not, but there are other things to consider.'

'Such as what?'

'My place in Parramatta is closer.'

His glance was startled. Hannah herself was startled at how much satisfaction she'd gained from the strong stance she'd just taken with Jack. During her marriage she'd always deferred meekly to Dwight. It was no wonder, perhaps, that he hadn't respected her. She would have Jack's respect, if it killed her.

'Let's make this a short visit,' he said, his glare having changed from surprised to smouldering.

Hannah, however, had no intention of rushing things, finding the feeling of anticipation about the night ahead acutely pleasurable.

'I wouldn't dream of offending Marion by racing away,' she said, eyes gleaming with suppressed desire. 'Besides,' she added on a husky breath, 'I don't want you having the time or the opportunity to make love to me again up here. I want to wait till I have you at home...in my bed.'

His blue eyes blazed, his own desire clearly unabated. 'I'll be ready to explode by then.'

'Mmm.'

'Witch,' he whispered under his breath as both of them heard Marion returning.

'You sure you've got that word right?' she whispered back, reaching up on tiptoe to give him a lightly teasing kiss.

His face said it all as Marion swept back into the room.

CHAPTER TWELVE

THE clock on the dashboard of Hannah's car showed ten past eight. It would probably be eight-thirty by the time they made it into the Marshall Homes car park—the same time most of the staff arrived. Hannah wished now that they'd started out earlier.

They were in the midst of heavy Monday morning traffic, just north of Parramatta, and a fine rain was falling, which always seemed to make the traffic worse. Hannah could never understand why it was that when it rained the number of cars on the road seemed to double. Maybe people who normally took public transport just couldn't face it in the rain.

She sighed when they slowed once again to a crawl.

'You've been very quiet this morning,' Jack said abruptly. 'Anything wrong?'

'I'm a little tired,' she said, which was true, but only half the story.

'You have only yourself to blame,' he said drily.

'I suppose so.' Her decision not to feel guilty about wanting Jack seemed to have given her an endless supply of energy last night, as well as a

167

desire to explore further ways of making love,
further ways of extending and heightening their
pleasure in each other. She'd revelled in taking
her time, and in making Jack take his, discover-
ing the sweet delights of a much slower surrender
to the passion they engendered in each other. It
had been after two in the morning by the time
they'd fallen asleep in each other's arms.

Hannah supposed that it wasn't any wonder
she felt a little under the weather this morning.
Five hours' sleep really wasn't enough.

But it wasn't the physical fatigue making her
quiet. It was the change in her feelings about what
she was doing. Maybe it was the cold light of
morning, or the rain, or the fact that they would
soon be at work, under the scrutiny of her
colleagues.

Hannah wasn't sure how she would handle the
situation if the people at Marshall Homes clued
on to the fact that the boss and his secretary had
become lovers. Jack was already exhibiting a
proprietorial and possessive attitude towards her
which she was sure would not go unnoticed. That,
combined with the fact that he'd broken his engagement to Felicia, would soon set tongues
wagging. It was impossible to keep such news a
secret.

She recalled what had happened when their last
sales manager—a married man—had started
having an affair with *his* secretary. Amazingly this
had seemed to give the man in question an added

status in some people's eyes. Ladies' men, for
some reason, were admired in certain quarters.
Lord knew why! The girl, however—who had
been only nineteen years old and very naïve—
had been labelled a fool and a slut. Hannah imagined that *she'd* be given some similar tags if
her affair with Jack became common knowledge—with a few more thrown in, given her age
and divorced status. It made her feel sick just
thinking about it.

'Jack...'

'What?'

'I...er...don't want people in the office to
know. You know...about us...'

They had just turned into the street which
housed the Marshall Homes head office, the two-
storeyed brick and glass complex just visible on
the hill in the far distance.

Jack slanted her a savage glance. 'I suppose I
can understand your wanting to keep our involvement a secret, Hannah. But, damn it all, I
don't like the way it makes me feel. I've never
had a woman ashamed of my being her lover. To
give Felicia credit, she knew how to make me feel
great all the time. Maybe there's something to be
said for getting mixed up with gold-diggers. At
least they always say what you want to hear.

'Do try not to run off the road,' he snapped.
'Yes, you don't have to say anything. I've got my
memory back. All of it.'

Hannah's hands clenched on the steering-wheel. 'When did this happen?' she asked, hating the way this news was affecting her. She knew in her heart that Jack would never go back to that woman, but she still detested being compared with her in any way.

'When I woke this morning everything was as clear as a bell,' he drawled, his tone implying that he was leaving a lot of things left unsaid.

'And?' she prompted.

'And pull over here,' he grated out. 'I'll walk the rest of the way. That way no one will see us together. I wouldn't want to embarrass you. And don't worry, when I walk in I won't grab you. I won't do a damned thing to raise anyone's suspicions that my poor put-upon secretary is providing her boss with more services than usual. I'll even wait till everyone else's gone home before I let my disgusting lust off the leash.'

Hannah's face flamed as she wrenched the car over to the kerb. She couldn't trust herself to say a word as he slammed out of the car and took off up the street with furious strides. She didn't turn her head as she drove past him. She didn't speak to him when he marched through her office into his. She was too busy hating him with all her heart.

When he stormed back out of the office ten minutes later, snapping that he wouldn't be back all day, she slumped down at her desk and burst into tears.

By ten she had the most excruciating headache behind her eyebrows. By eleven her throat felt as if it was lined with sandpaper. By noon she was running a temperature. She would have gone home if she'd had the energy. No doubt it was the flu. Most of the office had come down with it that winter at some time or other. It seemed it was her turn.

She swallowed some aspirin and stayed clammily at her desk, doing little but answer the telephone and take messages. The boys rang, as was their habit at lunchtime on a Monday, and she had to make a real effort to sound cheery. Nevertheless, she was relieved to hear that they hadn't heard from their father—either yesterday or as yet that day.

Not that she thought Dwight would say anything about their mother having a dirty weekend with her boss. His relationship with his sons didn't include telling them anything which was awkward or of an intimate nature. Hannah had done her best to explain the birds and the bees to them when they'd approached puberty, only to find that they already knew more than she did!

They had been less than impressed with their father having an affair—Hannah had managed to keep all his other affairs from their knowledge. She imagined that they wouldn't be thrilled with their mother doing the same, even if she *was* a divorcee. Sex, it seemed, was for other people.

Young people, not parents. And certainly not mothers!

Still, just in case Dwight was tempted to say something, she rang him at his surgery and asked him not to tell the boys about her involvement with Jack, impressing on her ex-husband that she wasn't about to marry Jack. That it was merely an affair. Oddly enough, he laughed.

'Just an affair?' he mocked. '*You*, Hannah? Don't be ridiculous. You've fallen in love with the man. Anyone with even the tiniest brain in their heads could see that. From what Felicia told me, you've been in love with him for ages!'

Hannah protested and finally hung up, even while the truth blasted into her feverish and maybe tiny brain. She *did* love Jack. She just hadn't recognised it, for it had been the love of a mature woman for a man—not the silly adolescent infatuation she'd once felt for Dwight and mistakenly called love. It was firmly based on all those emotions she'd already admitted to—liking and respect and, yes, gratitude. Jack had always been good to her—and kind, and decent.

His bringing to the surface her long-buried sexuality had confused to issue, that was all. She'd mistaken her obsessive desire for the man as something more superficial than a natural extension of a very real and deep affection, calling it lust, not love.

Yet it *was* love. *True* love.

After she had hung up, she sat there for ages, mulling over her astonishing realisation, shock gradually changing to a confused dismay. What should she do now? Tell Jack she'd changed her mind about marrying him? Tell him she loved him? Or tell him nothing?

Hannah still believed in her heart that marriage needed both partners to be in love with each other to be successful. But, given the situation she found herself in, she would rather marry Jack than go on being his secret lover. Respect was important to her, and what she was doing would inevitably erode Jack's respect for her, plus her respect for herself. On the other hand Jack had changed his mind about marriage yesterday. Then this morning he'd been none too pleased with her. Maybe she'd left it too late all round.

God, she couldn't think with her head throbbing away as it was. It was impossible.

Four-thirty slowly rolled around—the time the general office closed for the day. It wasn't uncommon for Hannah to work late, so no one commented when her light remained on, and her car stayed in the car park.

What the rest of the staff didn't know was that by this time Hannah felt too ill to drive home. She was lying down on the couch in Jack's well-appointed office, contemplating calling a taxi, when the man himself walked in, a sarcastic expression flitting across flinty eyes when he saw her.

'If your position is some kind of invitation,' he snarled, 'then I'm sorry, but I must decline. I'm too damned tired and not bloody interested! Nothing turns me off a woman more quickly than her being ashamed of being seen with me.'

Hannah squeezed her eyes tightly shut for a few seconds, Jack's derision having hit her hard. Yet she was beyond defending herself to him at that moment—beyond even reacting to his nasty outburst. She was beyond everything.

With a weary sigh she levered her feet over the side of the couch and stood up. Too quickly, as it turned out, her head spinning and her knees suddenly wobbly. She swayed, her right hand shooting out to grip the arm-rest of the couch for support, her left fluttering up in a vain attempt to dash the black spots away from her eyes.

She didn't actually faint. But she almost did; only Jack grabbing her and lowering her quickly back down on to the couch stopped its inevitability.

'Why didn't you tell me you were sick?' he groaned, stroking her hair gently back from her fevered brow. 'What is it? The flu? You're awfully hot.'

'I think so. I've been feeling rotten all day.'

He groaned again. 'I wish you'd told me. I wouldn't have been such a bastard if I'd known.'

She just looked at him, then turned her face away, a couple of tears sliding down her cheek.

'Geez, Hannah, don't make me feel more of a heel than I already do. Come on, let me take you upstairs. You're sleeping there for the night.' He bent and scooped her up into his arms as if she was a feather.

'And don't bother arguing with me,' he said as she stiffened and went to open her mouth. 'You're not fit to drive home. I'm going to get you into bed and then I'm going to call the doctor. This is no time for stupid displays of pride. You need looking after and I'm going to look after you.'

'I . . . I don't want to put you to any trouble,' she said weakly. 'Looking after sick people can be very tiresome. I might not be better for days, and I know you're busy, trying to finish the display village before spring.'

'If there's one thing last weekend taught me it's that the business won't fall apart if I take some time off. I've got good people working for me, Hannah. Marshall Homes will still be there next week.'

Hannah really had no energy to object to anything, so she lay back in Jack's arms and allowed him to carry her upstairs without further ado. She remained mute when he took her into the sleekly modern apartment, through the white and blue living-room and down the hallway into the master bedroom. When he sat her gently down on his big blue-quilted bed and began sliding the jacket of her tailored black suit from her shoulders, she sighed total acquiescence to his will.

His undressing her was oddly asexual, however, his touch not in any way seductive, merely gentle and concerned, his face similarly so. 'You're burning up, do you know that?' he said, once she was down to her black silk underwear. 'I think you should have a cooling shower. Are you strong enough? Good. I'll get you a clean T-shirt to wear to bed. Meanwhile I'm going to ring a doctor friend of mine to come and have a look at you. I don't think it's anything worse than flu, but I'm not taking any chances.'

Hannah was happy to follow his suggestions meekly, although she did faintly suggest that it might be better if she occupied the bed in the guest-room. Jack would have none of it, saying that his bed was king-sized and he wanted to be nearby in the night if she needed him.

She smiled wanly as her hot, aching head hit the pillow, hoping that the aspirin he'd given her would work quickly. Her eyes were beginning to water and her nose felt all stuffed up, with a vicious pain in her sinuses.

She wasn't feeling much better when Jack's doctor friend bustled in an hour later, apologising for not being able to come straight away. Marshall Homes had built his new home at Dural, Jack had told her while they were awaiting his arrival, in record time and to his demanding wife's satisfaction. It seemed the man felt somewhat in Jack's debt.

'So how is she?' Jack asked anxiously, once the doctor had completed his examination. 'It's just the flu, isn't it?'

'A particularly nasty case, but, yes, I think it's only flu.'

'I don't want you to just *think* so,' Jack snapped. 'I want you to be sure. My mother was diagnosed with the flu by a doctor and died two nights later from meningitis.'

'Hannah hasn't got meningitis, Jack. Sometimes the symptoms she's presenting can be a bad case of hay fever, combined with a simple cold. Did you perhaps spend some time on the weekend outdoors, Hannah?'

'Er...we did go for a bushwalk up in the Blue Mountains on Saturday,' she admitted, trying not to blush at the memories *that* evoked. 'But I've never had hay fever before.'

'There's always a first time. Are you a smoker?'

'Not any more, she isn't,' Jack muttered.

'I've not long given them up,' Hannah admitted.

'Well, don't go back on them if you can help it. Certainly not while you've got this virus. I'll prescribe you some antibiotics for your sinuses, plus some capsules combining antihistamines and painkillers. Really that's all that can be done at this stage.

'Stay in bed for at least two days,' he went on while he scribbled on a prescription pad, 'and drink plenty of fluids. And no going to work for the rest of the week. I would say by the weekend you'll be over the worst, and by next Monday you should be fighting fit again.'

'If she's not,' Jack said, in a darkly menacing tone, 'I know where you live.'

The doctor gave a rather nervous laugh as he looked up and handed him the two prescriptions. 'Very funny, Jack.'

'I don't have a sense of humour,' came the dry reply. 'Ask Hannah. She knows me better than anyone.'

'Only in the biblical sense,' Hannah muttered to herself while Jack ushered the harassed-looking doctor to the door.

'You weren't very nice to that poor man,' she reproved with a weary sigh when he returned. 'It was good of him to come as quickly as he did. Not many doctors make house-visits at all these days.'

'Maybe I'm just not feeling kind to doctors these days,' he grumbled. 'Look, I'll just dash out and get these scripts filled. The sooner we get some medicine into you, the better.'

He wasn't gone long, yet by the time he returned Hannah was on the verge of panic. Her head was killing her. She hoped she *didn't* have anything more serious than flu.

Jack frowned down at her. 'You look terrible. Here, get some of these into you.' He tipped out three capsules into the palm of her hand, then picked up the glass of water which he'd placed earlier on the bedside chest, holding it gently to her lips while she swallowed each pill. 'I'll go get some ice in a cloth,' he said, 'and cool your face down a bit.'

Hannah hated him leaving her alone, keeping her eyes glued to the doorway till he reappeared. Her gaze followed him as he strode back across the thick grey carpet. When he sat down on the bed and held the improvised ice-pack to her forehead, she sighed her satisfaction and closed her eyes. 'That feels wonderful,' she murmured.

'Don't talk,' he said, and began wiping the cool cloth over her forehead and head in a gently stroking fashion. 'Just rest. Go to sleep if you can.'

'Mmm.'

She did as she was told, but although she gradually began to feel a lot better, sleep eluded her. Finally she opened her eyes and gazed up into Jack's face. Knowing that she loved him seem to make him appear even more handsome to her now, his kind concern for her lending a softness to his hard-edged features.

'You must be tired of doing that,' she murmured.

'Not at all.'

'It feels lovely. I'm feeling much better. Thank you.'

'My pleasure.' And he smiled down at her.

Hannah's heart turned right over at that smile, for it was so sweet, and so utterly giving. She recalled how Dwight had always reacted with impatience to her ever being sick. He'd never stayed at home to look after her. Never showed her this kind of attention or caring.

There again, Dwight hadn't loved her...

'Oh!' She gasped as the implications of what she'd just thought blasted into her brain.

Jack's hand immediately whipped the cloth from her head, his eyes anxious upon her. 'What is it?' he demanded to know. 'Are you in pain? Hannah, darling, what is it?'

'You...you love me,' she said in a shocked whisper. 'I mean...you *really* love me.'

His expression became one of rueful tenderness. 'You've only just realised that, have you? Why do you think I asked you to marry me? Oh, yes, I know what you're probably going to say. A little over a week ago I asked Felicia to marry me, and I certainly didn't love *her*!'

He dropped the cloth next to her glass of water and returned to stroke her damp hair back from her face with his hand, his feathery touch infinitely tender and loving. 'I think I've been falling in love with you since the first day I interviewed you, Hannah, only I didn't realise it. Or maybe

I did,' he revised. 'Subconsciously. But I didn't think I had a chance in hell with you.

'I guess my own personal survival instinct kept a firm hand on my private desires where you were concerned, so that I didn't make a fool of myself. Yet I still made a fool of myself—letting Felicia sway me with her flattery and her lies.

'Losing my memory the way I did was the best thing that could have happened to me. With that lying manipulative bitch out of my head, and you suddenly being receptive to me in a sexual sense, my true feelings for you began to surface with a vengeance.

'I've never wanted a woman before as I wanted you this weekend, believe me. But it was more than sex, Hannah. It was a compulsion—an obsessive need to stamp my possession on you as my woman. And I succeeded in some small way, didn't I? I know you don't love me the same way I love you, but I think you——'

'But I *do*!' she broke in, grabbing his hand and pulling herself up into a sitting position. 'I love you so much I've been in the depths of despair all day!'

He seemed even more shocked than when she'd told him last Friday that she was his fiancée.

'I...I refused to marry you because I didn't think you really loved me,' she hastened to explain, not wanting to tell him that she hadn't realised her own feelings till lunchtime today, or that it had been Dwight who'd finally made her see the truth. Jack deserved better than that. 'Oh, darling,' she said, cupping his face and gazing adoringly into his eyes. 'I'd kiss you if I wasn't afraid I'd give you germs.'

'God, Hannah. I can't tell you how happy you've just made me.' And he hugged her fiercely, almost squeezing all the breath out of her. 'I'm never going to let you go, my darling. Never.'

'If you don't,' she whispered weakly, 'I might just expire from suffocation.'

He swiftly let her go, then fussed over her some more, lying her back on the pillows and apologising profusely. For her part Hannah no longer cared about her flu, or whatever it was she had. Happiness seemed to be a wonderful and almost instant cure. Or was it love? Love, she decided dazedly, could cure anything—most of all the hurts of the past.

'We're going to be so happy together,' Jack vowed fiercely. 'I'm going to build us a fantastic house to live in down here, and another one up in the mountains. That cold, mouldy old cottage just has to go!'

'The houses that Jack built?' she said, teasing lights gleaming in her eyes.

'Trust you to say that, Miss Smarty-pants,' he growled. 'You'd better watch it, madam, or I won't give you any of those little *bambinos* everyone says you'll want.'

She sat bolt-upright again. 'But I thought you didn't want children!'

'Where on earth did you get such a stupid idea?'

'From you!'

'Yeah, well, I was wrong, wasn't I? I realised how wrong I was the moment I held that cute little possum in my arms. I reckon I'd make a good father after all.'

Hannah's eyes began to water even more than they already had been. 'You'd make a great father, Jack.' Which was true. He'd been fantastic with Chris and Stuart during their last holidays, the boys having taken to him straight away. Hannah had no doubt that her sons would really like Jack as their stepfather.

'I guess my own father dumping my mother when he found out she was pregnant rather jaundiced my idea of fatherhood,' Jack explained. 'That, combined with all those lonely years I spent in the orphanage after my mother died, turned me into a bit of a loner.

'I trained myself into not needing or loving anyone. I guess it got to be a habit till I hired a certain secretary and she began to show me what a woman's love could mean. It sent me off looking for the wrong kind of love for a while, but she eventually got me back on track.'

'I shudder to think what would have happened if that tile hadn't fallen on you,' Hannah said, shaking her head. 'We might never have known how much we loved each other.'

'Oh, yes, we would,' Jack pronounced firmly. 'I didn't call off my engagement to Felicia just because of her apparent involvement with Gerald Boynton. I didn't like the way she treated you at the party that night. Don't think I didn't notice. I couldn't help comparing the two women in my life and knowing instinctively which one I preferred. I'd already decided by the time that night ended to start pushing the issue with you. I was going to start slowly, because I knew you'd been hurt in your first marriage, but then that tile fell on my head, and things happened very quickly indeed.'

'Maybe too quickly,' Hannah murmured.

'Hell, no. The quicker the better at our age. If I can ever find that title I'm going to have it bronzed! Now, try to get some sleep, darling,' he said. 'I want you getting better as quickly as possible.'

'If I'm to stay here, you... you'll have to go over to my place in the morning and get me some things. Especially my pill.'

'Why don't you stop taking that?' he suggested softly.

'You mean that, Jack?'

'We're not getting any younger.'

'True.'

'Do you think Marion and Edward would like to be godparents to our first child?'

'They'd be ecstatic.'

'They'll make excellent babysitters when we need them, won't they?'

'More than excellent.'

'We can leave any little *bambinos* with them, and sneak off by ourselves occasionally.'

'Mmm. That sounds good.'

'Are you sure I'll get germs if I kiss you?' he asked thickly.

'Yes.'

'What if I don't kiss your mouth? What if I concentrate on other parts of you?'

'You're incorrigible.'

'Must you use such big words?'

Hannah smiled up at him.

'I think I'll go back to stroking your forehead,' Jack said wryly. 'I know if I start any of that nonsense I won't want to stop.'

'There's always tomorrow, Jack.'

'I suppose so.'

'And every other day for the rest of our lives.'

His face brightened appreciably. 'What a lovely thought.'

'It is, isn't it?'

'I still can't believe you love me,' he said, choking up. 'I don't deserve you.'

'You deserve the best, my darling.'

'I have the best,' he said, and dropped a kiss on her forehead.

'Oh, Jack...' She looked up at him, eyes swimming.

'Bugger the germs,' he growled, and his mouth began to descend.

* * * * *

If you enjoyed Hannah and Jack's story, then look out for next month's final romance in Miranda Lee's beguiling new trilogy

AFFAIRS TO REMEMBER.

Coming next month:

A WOMAN TO REMEMBER

When Luke St Clair meets a mystery blonde and has a one-night affair with her, she is imprinted on his memory forever. Whoever she is, Luke cannot forget her and, two years later, scours the whole of Sydney to find her. It takes cunning, trickery and the power of passion to bring Rachel back into Luke's life, but then he begins to wonder if he is the one who has been used...!

AFFAIRS TO REMEMBER: stories of love you'll treasure forever.

MILLS & BOON

Just *Married*

Celebrate the joy, excitement and adjustment that comes with being 'Just Married' in this wonderful collection of four new short stories.

Written by four popular authors

Sandra Canfield

Muriel Jensen

Elise Title

Rebecca Winters

Just Married is guaranteed to melt your hearts— just married or not!

Available: April 1996   Price: £4.99

MILLS & BOON

Today's Woman

Mills & Boon brings you a new series of seven
fantastic romances by some of your favourite
authors. One for every day of the week in fact
and each featuring a truly wonderful woman
who's story fits the lines of the old rhyme
'Monday's child is...'

Look out for Patricia Knoll's
Desperately Seeking Annie in April '96.

Thursday's child Annie Parker is recovering
from amnesia when she meets a tall dark
handsome stranger who claims to be her
husband. But how can she spend the rest of her
life with a man she can't even remember—
let alone remember marrying?

Temptation

Coming up in
BACHELOR ARMS...

When Blythe Fielding planned her wedding and asked her two best friends, Caitlin and Lily, to be bridesmaids, none of them had a clue a new romance was around the corner for each of them—even the bride!

These entertaining, dramatic stories of friendship, mystery and love by **JoAnn Ross** continue to follow the exploits of the residents of Bachelor Arms. If you loved the male Bachelor Arms titles you'll love the next set coming up in Temptation featuring the female residents of this lively apartment block.

Look out for:

FOR RICHER OR POORER (March 1996)
THREE GROOMS AND A WEDDING (April 1996)

GET 4 BOOKS AND A MYSTERY GIFT

FREE

Return this coupon and we'll send you 4 Mills & Boon Romances and a mystery gift absolutely FREE! We'll even pay the postage and packing for you.

We're making you this offer to introduce you to the benefits of Reader Service: FREE home delivery of brand-new Mills & Boon romances, at least a month before they are available in the shops, FREE gifts and a monthly Newsletter packed with information.

Accepting these FREE books and gift places you under no obligation to buy, you may cancel at any time, even after receiving just your free shipment. Simply complete the coupon below and send it to:

MILLS & BOON READER SERVICE, FREEPOST, CROYDON, SURREY, CR9 3WZ.

No stamp needed

Yes, please send me 4 free Mills & Boon Romances and a mystery gift. I understand that unless you hear from me, I will receive 6 superb new titles every month for just £2.10* each postage and packing free. I am under no obligation to purchase any books and I may cancel or suspend my subscription at any time, but the free books and gifts will be mine to keep in any case. (I am over 18 years of age)

1EP6R

Ms/Mrs/Miss/Mr _____

Address _____

_____

_____ Postcode _____

Offer closes 30th September 1996. We reserve the right to refuse an application. *Prices and terms subject to change without notice. Offer only valid in UK and Ireland and is not available to current subscribers to this series. **Readers in Ireland please write to: P.O. Box 4546, Dublin 24.** Overseas readers please write for details.

mps MAILING PREFERENCE SERVICE

You may be mailed with offers from other reputable companies as a result of this application. Please tick box if you would prefer not to receive such offers. ☐

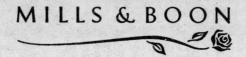

MILLS & BOON

Next Month's Romances

Each month you can choose from a wide variety of romance with Mills & Boon. Below are the new titles to look out for next month.

HOT BLOOD	Charlotte Lamb
PRISONER OF PASSION	Lynne Graham
A WIFE IN WAITING	Jessica Steele
A WOMAN TO REMEMBER	Miranda Lee
SPRING BRIDE	Sandra Marton
DESPERATELY SEEKING ANNIE	Patricia Knoll
THE BACHELOR CHASE	Emma Richmond
TAMING A TYCOON	Leigh Michaels
PASSION WITH INTENT	Natalie Fox
RUTHLESS!	Lee Wilkinson
MY HERO	Debbie Macomber
UNDERCOVER LOVER	Heather Allison
REBEL BRIDE	Sally Carr
SECRET COURTSHIP	Grace Green
PERFECT STRANGERS	Laura Martin
HEART'S REFUGE	Quinn Wilder

Available from WH Smith, John Menzies, Volume One, Forbuoys, Martins, Woolworths, Tesco, Asda, Safeway and other paperback stockists.